WVP

Ⓑ

HIGH VALLEY RIVER

Romer Zane Grey

Zane Grey's legendary hero Buck Duane is back in this pair of adventures written by his son. When a dying man gasps out a desperate message to the Texas Ranger, Buck is sent on a lonely mission to High Valley and discovers a plot to destroy the ranches there. In the end, his guns wipe out the ruthless killers. Then it's on to northern Texas to clean out a band of rustlers. As tough as they are, they're no match for Buck Duane!

Also by Romer Zane Grey
in Large Print

KING OF THE RANGE

THE OTHER SIDE OF
  THE MOUNTAIN

Romer Zane Grey

HIGH VALLEY RIVER

John Curley & Associates, Inc.
South Yarmouth, Ma.

Library of Congress Cataloging in Publication Data

Grey, Romer.
  High Valley River.

  1. Large type books.   I. Title.
[PS3557.R485H5   1983]   813'.54   82–22180
ISBN 0–89340–555–8

Published in Large Print by arrangement with Singer Communications Inc.

Distributed in the U.K. and Commonwealth by Magna Print Books.

Printed in Great Britain

HIGH VALLEY RIVER

Chapter I

At the crowded San Antonio Hotel bar the big man was as alone as if still riding the range in his high, West Texas home. His brow was furrowed by thought, and his weathered face set in lines of increasing determination. Suddenly he set his half emptied glass on the bar and turned away towards the door to the street.

It was all over in an instant. The big fellow pushed open the swinging doors and stepped into the street. It was as if he'd walked head on into an invisible barrier. The force of the heavy, forty-five caliber slug stopped him in his tracks and stiffened every nerve and muscle with shock. His six-foot body slammed back against the door frame and then fell, half over the sill.

In the howling hullabaloo of a San Antonio Saturday night few people even heard the shot. No one noticed who had fired.

Three or four of the more responsible

business men in the hotel bar left their drinking and ran over to where the shot man lay, still paralyzed by the shock of his wound.

"He's not dead yet," one of them said. "Sam, you run see if Doc Willis is in his office."

"He'll be dead soon," Sam replied, "but I'll go anyhow." He ran out the door.

The wounded man had been shot through the stomach. Given the terrible smashing power of a forty-five and the still primitive medical techniques of the late nineteenth century frontier, he hadn't a chance to survive. They knew it even as they tried to make him more comfortable.

It was obvious, as the shock wore off a little, that he knew it too.

"Rangers," he said in a hoarse, feeble voice. "I got to talk to Rangers."

"Take it easy, man," somebody said. "Save your strength. The doc'll be here quick." They were wadding bar towels to try to stanch the terrible wounds, front and back of his body. It wasn't much use.

"Doc h – " the man said weakly. "Too late for a doc. Ranger . . . Ranger . . ."

A short wiry man with the look of command in his keen, intelligent grey eyes

4

pushed through the crowd in the doorway.

"Give me room," he said, and men fell back instinctively. "It's all right, mister," he said. "It's okay. I'm a Ranger. MacNelly's my name. You can tell me whatever is it."

"Thank God," the man gasped, "but alone."

"Move him into one of the ground floor rooms," Captain MacNelly commanded. "Send in the doc when he gets here – and hurry up. Time's running fast for this man."

Men who owned their own ranches and stores jumped to obey the little man. They knew authority when they met it face to face.

"He died all right," Captain MacNelly said the next morning in his sparsely furnished office in the San Antonio Ranger barracks.

"He died hard though, and it gave him time to talk. He wasn't afraid any more, so he said all he could."

"I know," the man sitting in the plain kitchen chair in front of the bare oak table which served the Captain for a desk said slowly. "When a man sees old-skull-and-bones in the door it will unlock his tongue. I suppose it's a job for us."

"A job for you, Buck," MacNelly said. "He told enough for me to know there's something badly wrong up in his country, but not enough for me to know exactly what. Towards the end there his mind was wandering, and some of the things he said weren't exactly clear. Some of them sounded downright crazy."

"You want me to take in a squad and find out?" Buck Duane asked.

"I want you to take yourself in, Buck. No squad, no badge even. The dead man was mighty emphatic about that. If a Texas Ranger even shows himself up that way, he told me, why then it's all up with his friends."

"What would happen then?" Buck Duane asked.

"You won't believe me, but I'll give it to you in his own words. Just about his last words they were too. Mr. Smith will kill the river, he said. Just like that – Mr. Smith will kill the river."

"If he can kill a river," Duane said, "this Smith must ride mighty tall in the saddle. You're right, Captain. It doesn't make sense."

"It had better make sense," MacNelly said, "when you come out of High Valley City, Buck. Somebody up there has the town in his hand and the ranchers in fear of

6

death. After last night I can see how come they're scared. Murder and all, it's Ranger business. After I tell you what I know I want you to go up there and find Mr. Smith and what he's up to and bring him out."

There was silence in the room for a moment. Then MacNelly scratched a big sulphur match on his boot sole and lit a long black cigar.

"Finding a Smith ought to be easy," Duane said with a grin. "First and last there's more hombres calling themselves Smith in Texas than in the whole rest of the States. Always has been a popular name with gents racing some sheriff from back home. Only how do I know which is the right Smith, Cap? Am I looking for a lame Mr. Smith, or a gotch-eared Smith or a Mr. Bob Smith or what?"

"You're looking for a Mr. Smith who can sit five hundred miles away in High Valley and kill a man in the Austin Hotel in San Antonio in just two minutes after that man decides to come to see the Rangers," MacNelly said. "That's the kind of Mr. Smith you're looking for, and that's all I know. Near as the dead man could say, there ain't nobody in High Valley has even seen Mr. Smith. They know he's there all right,

7

because he kills anybody don't take his orders meek as a lamb – but nobody sees him."

"I'm one lamb ain't quite that meek," Duane said. "If he's alive, I'll bring in Mr. Smith for you."

"Now that's the kind of talk I like to hear," MacNelly said. "I knew I could count on you, Buck. Now listen close while I tell you all I can. In the morning you can ride."

"In the morning I ride," Buck Duane said. He pulled his chair closer to the table.

Chapter II

High noon found Buck Duane and his mount Bullet well on the roads that led west and north from San Antonio into the high country of West Texas. The big man sat his saddle easily with the air born of a lifetime on horseback. He wore no badge except the two big guns holstered low and tied down by rawhide thongs around the worn woolen trouser legs and the Winchester in its saddle boot.

The pack horse he led bore no official brand. Only an observer who noted the beautiful grace of his steel-muscled body and his air of unwavering alertness to all about him would have guessed that this was a man who had ridden the outlaw trails for a decade before joining the Rangers. Only one who had looked into his steel grey eyes could know what sort of man Buck Duane really was.

He pushed his horse steadily onwards, sleeping in hospitable ranch houses, small town hotels or under the clean, high-riding stars, depending upon where the evening found him.

As he rode his mind was busy weighing and considering the few facts which Captain MacNelly had been able to give him concerning his mission.

Buck Duane had never been to High Valley City. His outlaw days had been spent in the country further south and nearer to the Rio Grande.

He'd heard of the place, of course, as sooner or later the verbal grapevine of the frontier brought him news of all sorts of places and people.

The town was young, even for the raw frontier of Texas. It had been settled largely in the past five or six years. Men spoke well of the country in which it lay. The valley was called high, but actually it was in a range of rolling hills at the edge of a much higher escarpment.

The land was said to be good, carpeted with prairie and buffalo grass and watered by the High Valley River, which came down from the loftier hills to the west. There was cottonwood along the river and evergreens further up. It should have been – and as far as anyone in San Antonio knew – it was an ideal ranching country.

The papers on the dead man identified him as William Bass, rancher in the valley and owner of the registered W-B brand. Duane's ostensible errand was to carry news of the man's death, return his valuables to any survivors and report his burial in San Antonio.

He'd decided to pass himself off as a potential buyer of a ranch of his own. It would give him a perfectly logical 'cover' for as long as he wanted to remain in the Valley, ride over the land and ask questions.

It should also provide a position of standing that a mere saddlebum or a fugitive from justice would lack.

He'd use his own name, talk to as many ranchers as he could reach, and keep alert for any sign of the mysterious Mr. Smith.

Later on, when he knew what it was that Bass had feared so greatly and what 'killing a river' actually meant, he could either reveal his true identity as a Ranger or send for Captain MacNelly and a troop if he felt that any help would be needed.

In any case, he'd start out as a prospective land and cattle buyer and play it by ear from there on in.

The last night before reaching High Valley City Buck Duane made a dry camp in a clump of cottonwoods along the bank of the High Valley River itself. It was a peaceful summer night with the tall grass blowing and the leaves of the trees shifting and whispering in the wind. The sun-warmed ground was firm under his blankets and the high-riding moon showered the prairie with silver light so bright a man could have a read fine print if he'd had a book with him.

Duane did not. He lay on top of his blanket with his head pillowed on Bullet's saddle and thought about the job ahead. Duane knew himself competent to handle just about any situation that might arise. Long years on the owlhoot trail had taught him things that most men never knew. His wits and his guns had been the match for enemies before, yet he knew enough never to indulge in the luxury of overconfidence.

Someone, not far away, had woven a net of evil. There was a body under a plain wooden cross in San Antonio to prove how deadly that menace could be and how far its murderous reach extended. The same danger would be directed against Buck Duane if he made the slightest slip in judgment or in action – and well he knew no man was proof against a murderer's bullet.

More shaking than anything else was the element of mystery involved. A Texas Ranger was used to going against long odds. He lived by danger as another man did by bread. But this was against known enemies and odds that could be calculated in advance, long as they might prove to be.

"An enemy understood is already half beaten," had been one of Buck Duane's personal sayings for as long as he could remember. He'd learned it at the knee of his father, that legendary gunslinger whose name still made men pause in fear and who had been a name to conjure with before the guns of ambush cut him down.

Tomorrow though, Duane would ride against an unknown enemy and odds which he could not name. Instead of a man of flesh and blood it was a shadow which he chased this time. He couldn't plan against a faceless, formless evil. He could only wait and maintain ceaseless vigilance.

At last Duane closed his eyes and slept. It is a measure of the man that no nightmare haunted his rest and that he woke refreshed at the first lark call of daybreak.

The town, when he first spotted it from a

slight rise of the road, showed nothing to indicate the presence of a lurking menace of any sort.

There was the usual half mile of one story false-fronted frame buildings: stores, saloons and the few professional offices needed to serve a cattle town. Back of this, small frame homes clustered along the river bank under cottonwood trees which cut the sun's heat.

There were a few larger buildings on higher ground to house the leading citizens. There was the white wooden spire of a church – and a little way out of town a building that just had to be the familiar one room school with a big iron triangle hanging from posts in the yard to summon students in place of a bell. That was all.

The river ran close by the town. It was a good hundred feet wide, flowing fast over a rocky bed and with what looked like a deep channel in the center. There was no bridge, so it had to be fordable by horse or wagon.

Duane headed straight for a building which proclaimed *Restaurant* in bright red paint on a newly made sign. He knew well enough what sort of meal he'd have to make do with if he took the only other choice of eating place and stopped at the saloon.

14

A motherly looking woman at the restaurant served him boiled hominy with redeye gravy, fried eggs, country ham and gossip, all in heaping portions. She also tried to question him on news of the world outside.

Between mouthfuls of the savoury food Buck Duane gave her news from the East, being careful to omit any references to the murder of the late Mr. Bass.

She told him herself that "Bill Bass went on to San Antone to buy supplies." His ranch, it seemed, was north and west of town towards Sweetwater Gap where the river comes down.

"Yes – there was a lawyer in town. Warn't likely he'd wake up till noon though. No, she didn't know of any ranch for sale."

In all of her talk there was no mention of anyone by the name of Smith, or any indication of menace hanging over the area. Of course she was new in town herself – the paint hardly dry on her business sign – and that might account for it.

After eating Duane went up the street to the office of 'Judge' Gowanus, the town's single attorney at law. The legal eagle had just risen from the couch in his office where he slept and opened the door clad only in a suit of dirty cotton 'long john' underwear.

Sight of a client, or at least a stranger who might turn out to be a client, worked miracles in a matter of minutes. After a long snort of whiskey and a short one from the water pitcher, Gowanus climbed into a reasonably clean shirt and pants, got his boots on and offered Duane a drink and a chair.

The first thing Buck Duane did was to offer to turn over the small packet of Bass's personal possessions which "the San Antone authorities asked me to bring on up, since I was coming along anyway."

"Old Bill Bass dead?" Gowanus looked considerably startled. "What happened? Get himself in a fight?"

"No fight," Duane said. "At least that ain't what I heard. Wasn't there myself of course. Seems like somebody unknown just shot him down in cold blood when he was leaving his hotel. Wouldn't know if he had any enemies down there, would you?"

"Who, me?" Gowanus looked scared to death himself. "How would I know about anything that far off? What do you want to know fer anyway?"

"No reason," Duane said easily. "Just curiosity."

The lawyer poured out what was left in the whiskey bottle. It filled the one tumbler halfway, and he drank it down at one gulp. It didn't seem to steady him much.

"Well, don't get so curious," he snapped at Duane. "Feller gets killed, it's best leave it alone less'n you're a sheriff or som'at."

"Not me," Buck Duane said.

"Okay then. Leave it be. Terrible thing though. Nice feller like Bill. Goes off on a business trip and next thing you bring back his wallet. He live long after the shooting?" He shot a sly glance at Duane and then fumbled in a desk drawer and brought up another bottle.

"I wouldn't know," Duane said. "I told you I wasn't there."

"Oh, so you did. So you did. Now look here, friend, whyn't you carry that stuff out to the W-B yourself? His widow'll likely have questions and you know more about it than I do. Sides, I hate riding in the hot sun. Anybody in town kin direct you."

"Since you suggest it," Duane said, "I'll do just that. Now for my own business – I'm thinking of buying a ranch up this way. You know about anything available?"

Gowanus gave himself time for another drink before answering. The liquor was

17

beginning to take effect. He gave Duane a long, owlish stare.

"Want to buy a ranch," he inquired. "Well you ain't the first to say that, not yet the last to regret it. Look like a handy sort of chap with those guns though, so why shouldn't you buy a ranch?"

"I asked about land," Duane said.

"So you did. So you did, mister. Well, for the matter of that there's plenty land. Plenty government land for a man to take up. Land and water." He laughed to himself and cocked his head at Duane. "On the other hand, if you really want land, why then the man to see is Ace Holden. Yes, you go see Ace."

"Why him?"

"Because I said so," Gowanus said. "You do or you don't – I can't care less. Now go on get out of here and let a man drink his breakfast in peace. Go on, I said."

Buck Duane left. "He knows more about Bass' killing than he wants to let on," he told himself. "He's scared by it, and I'd like to know why."

The only hotel in town was also the saloon and gambling house. *Ace Holden, Prop.* the sign outside said. Duane knew there'd be little rest or sleep for anyone taking a room there. The bar would be open all night.

Down at the far end of the street he found a neat white clapboards two-story house with a sign that said simply *Rooms*.

The landlady was a handsome woman in her forties with warm brown eyes and her hair tied back in a bun. She gave the handsome, lean muscled rider an appreciative glance and showed him to a clean, comfortable room in the ground floor rear not far from the kitchen.

"Three dollars a week," she said. "You want board, it'll be three more."

Buck Duane sniffed the odor of biscuits coming from the kitchen and his face warmed with a rare smile.

"I'll want board," he said.

The woman smiled back and made to close the door. Then she remembered.

"In advance," she said.

Duane gave her six dollars. He left his saddle bags in the room and took both horses down the street to the one livery stable.

"Keep the pack beast here," he told the owner. "Just feed and water the big roan. I'm riding out a ways this afternoon, but I'll bring him back tonight."

Chapter III

While Bullet was being cared for, Buck Duane went down the street to Ace Holden's combined hotel, bar and gambling house.

He stood up to the forty-foot long mahogany bar and ordered beer. The bar was expensive and the big mirror on the wall behind it must have cost a fortune to haul this far west.

"Nice place," he told the bartender.

"You can bet on that," the man said. "Ace – he's the owner – likes to do things right. Yessiree. Nothing but the best for Ace."

"Sounds like a real sport," Buck Duane said.

"You can bet on it," the bartender said. "Even got a pool table in the back room. Real ivory balls. Come all the way from Afrikee, they did. And say, mister. You come back tonight when the girls has got their paint on and come downstairs. You just do that. Fanciest girls in a thousand miles, Ace says. They knows tricks you never even heard of. Just you see." He wiped the bar with his rag and went to another customer.

Buck Duane took his time over the beer, but no one who might have been Ace Holden came into the room. He decided to ride on out to the Bass ranch and see the gambler later.

It wasn't much of a ride. The ranch house was only a few miles north of town and close to the river. It sat comfortably under the shade of big cottonwoods.

Mrs. Bass herself, a matronly woman about the same age as the dead man, met Duane at the door of the house. When he began to work up to his errand she guessed it right away and asked him into the big, homey kitchen to sit down.

Buck Duane broke the news as kindly as he could.

"It was just one shot," he said. "He died right off. Possibly he never even knew he'd been hit."

He thought that might comfort her, and besides, MacNelly had warned him not to let on how much the man had talked.

She took it bravely with the innate courage and natural dignity which ennobled so many ranch wives and mothers on the far frontier. Her face set in a cruel mask of calm, but Duane could see the pulse beat quicken and throb at her throat as she fought to control any visible display of the emotion which wracked her within.

"It's easier that we had no children," she said, half to herself. "To lose a father would have made things so hard for them. A woman alone can manage – ."

Duane couldn't help asking: "Just what do you plan to do, Mrs. Bass?"

"I'll manage," she said. "William had a little money in the San Antonio bank. That's why he went all that way to do business. It'll be enough to take me back to Ohio. I've a married sister there; and perhaps a little restaurant or sewing to help out – ." Her voice trailed off.

"You've got a fine ranch here," Buck Duane said. "I couldn't help but notice as I rode in. Surely, even if you don't care to stay on, it'll fetch a good price for you. Enough to put into a good business back east?"

Mrs. Bass gave him a level look.

"Oh, no," she said. "But of course you're a stranger and don't know. It isn't that easy her in High Valley. I can sell, but not at my price. But now – I don't mean to impose upon your kindness in coming to see me. Let me fix a pot of coffee, Mr. Duane."

"You aren't imposing, though I will accept the coffee. What you just said interests me for another reason. I've just come into a bit of money myself. The real reason I came out to this part of Texas in the first place was to look for a small ranch for myself. If you do decide to sell – and your spread here proves out as good as it looks to me now – you might not have to depend on finding a local buyer."

Mrs. Bass was bustling about the stove, and kept her face averted from his eyes.

"That's real nice of you to say, Mr. Duane. If things were different I might maybe talk business with you. But there's special things here in the valley. Please just take my word for it."

"I wish you'd explain," Duane said. When she kept stubbornly silent he went on, "I really do like the looks of this valley. If you don't sell me your land, I'm sure I can find somebody else that will. I'm willing to pay a fair price."

She took down two large, blue willow-pattern cups and saucers and set them on the table. Next to the cups went a small plate holding a brown cone of sugar to be dipped in the hot drink and a crock of thick cream.

"I think," Buck Duane said, "it'd only be fair if you told me what you meant just now. I'm honestly interested."

"Maybe you are," she said. "I kind of like you and I think you could be honest, but you're a stranger. In this place we don't talk open like to strangers. It ain't healthy."

She caught a sob in her throat and Duane knew she was thinking of her husband. In a moment she had control of herself again.

"No. It ain't always healthy, Mr. Duane. If you insist on staying round here long, you'll find out for yourself. I wish you'd just ride on while you can. I truly do. I'll make out all right."

Buck Duane said: "You owe me more explanation than that, Mrs. Bass. I am a stranger, just like you say. If there's something I'll find out anyway, don't you think it better I should hear from friendly lips first – and know what it is I'll be up against?"

She poured the coffee for them both and set out cold biscuits, fresh sweet butter and a glass of homemade jelly. Her resolve seemed to be weakening.

"I don't know," she said. "I honestly don't know."

Duane pushed his advantage. "I'm a man

24

grown, Mrs. Bass. When I know the facts I can make a decision what to do. But not before I know. I'm a free man and I can take care of myself."

He realized right away that had been the wrong thing to say.

Her control broke completely for the first time. She put both elbows down on the table, buried her face in her hands and shook with great sobs.

"Oh, Mr. Duane," she managed finally, "I'm sorry. Truly I'm sorry. It's just that my Bill always used to say that. He could take care of himself. He was so proud of that. And now – ."

Buck Duane had to fight down the impulse to say to her: "He did take care of you. He lived to say enough to bring me here." He knew it would be a comfort, but he dared not talk as yet. Perhaps, later on if she came to trust him . . . But first he had to know if she had summoned up the courage to defy the nameless menace that hung over this beautiful valley. To talk too soon would be to betray the mission upon which Captain MacNelly had sent him.

All he could say was: "I'm sorry."

"I know you are," she said. "Somehow I

feel it. Maybe later on, when I've had time to think, when the shock of hearing about Mr. Bass has worn off. Like I say, maybe then." She couldn't finish.

Duane got to his feet. "I'm sorry, Mrs. Bass. I should have remembered how you must feel. I'll ride along now. I am really interested in this ranch though, if you do decide to sell. Later on, when you feel better, I'll stop by again and talk to you about it. Meantime, if you change your mind, I've taken a room at Mrs. Burke's in town. You can reach me there."

She wiped her eyes. "At Sally Burke's? That's good. She runs a nice clean house and the meals'll stick to your ribs."

She walked to the door with him. Just as he was about to leave she put a hand on his elbow. "Mr. Duane, maybe I shouldn't say anything at all more right now. I just can't help it though. You've been so considerate. A real gentleman. I've said too much already as it is. Still, you just remember this one thing.

"To buy or sell land in High Valley. It don't matter either way. There's just one man you have to see. One man only. You mark what I say now – and I just hope I'm

26

not saying too much. But I feel like somehow I owed it to you – ."

She paused.

"Yes, Mrs. Bass," Duane said.

"You got to go see that man." She paused again and then seemd to gather her courage. "It's Ace Holden," she said. "You want to stay in town more'n overnight you make your peace with Ace Holden. Nobody buys or sells without he gives the word. That's all."

Buck Duane bowed and went down the two steps to the hardpacked, clean-swept yard.

"Thank you, Mrs. Bass," he said. "I'll remember. Thank you again for telling me."

His mind was full of other questions as he rode slowly back towards the river. Why Ace Holden? Didn't the ranchers own their land? What about "Mr. Smith"? Was Holden just another name for Smith?" Nobody's mentioned that name yet. What could Ace Holden do to Mrs. Bass if she sold against his will? There were a lot of answers Buck Duane needed to know.

Some of the Bass cattle were grazing near the ranch-house itself. They looked well fed and healthy. They all bore the W-B brand, but some of the other and older steers bore an additional brand. That was normal enough when a man had bought grown steers. He'd naturally add his own brand.

What was unusual to Duane's trained and experienced eye was that some of the original brands had obviously been changed and reworked with a hot iron. He rode as close as he could to the grazing steers to make sure his eyes hadn't betrayed him. They hadn't.

"Those brands have been changed," Duane told Bullet and patted the big horse's neck. "Bass wouldn't do that. He might cross out the old brand with a swipe of the iron before putting on his W Bar B. Lots of men do that, but only a rustler reworks a brand. Now I'm sure Bass and his wife ain't rustlers, and they don't seem the sort to buy stolen stock from them that steals it."

He sat his horse for a while and watched the cattle move about.

"Some of them are Texas steers," he thought. "On the other hand some look like they was bred south of the Rio Grande. How would Mex steers get up this way?"

After a while he filed the questions in his mind and rode on into town.

Chapter IV

The dinner at Sally Burke's boarding house was as savory and good as Mrs. Bass had predicted. There were only three other boarders. One was a middle-aged spinster who taught at the town school. The second was a younger man who clerked in the drygoods store and the third a traveling whiskey salesman from St. Louis.

The drummer did most of the talking; answered mostly in monosyllables by the clerk and Mrs. Burke. The school teacher gave an occasional dissapproving sniff, but Buck Duane noticed she had an appetite like a man and really shoveled in the roast beef and potatoes that came to the table on heaped ironstone platters.

After eating, the teacher retired to her room and the three men took chairs on the long wooden porch that fronted the house. The other two lit cigars.

Buck Duane had learned not to smoke during his long years on the outlaw side of the law. Tobacco was hard to come by and an unsatisfied craving was bad for a man alone. Besides, the smell of smoke could give a man away to a pursuer. It was easier to chew, as some outlaws did, or not to smoke at all. He put his feet up on the rail, tipped back his chair and pretended to doze while the others talked.

For a time he could hear Mrs. Burke moving about and clattering dishes in the kitchen. When he judged by the sounds that her chores were nearly done he walked back through the house and drew himself a glass of water from the small pump at the sink.

"That was a fine meal," he said appreciatively.

Sally Burke untied her apron and hung it on a nail. Together they stepped out under the shade of the giant cottonwood tree in the rear yard. Dusk had fallen and a cool breeze blew up from the river. Fireflies made glowing spots of light. The moon had not yet climbed up over the eastern horizon. It was a quiet and friendly moment, and both of them savored it.

"You interest me, Buck Duane," she said. She was a tall woman and her head came a bit higher than his shoulder. She wasn't looking at him as she spoke.

"Thank you," he said.

"Don't misunderstand me," she said then, still not looking directly at him. Her hair blew a little in the breeze where it had come loose from the bun. "Of course you interest me as a man does a woman alone. That wasn't what I meant."

Both of them were silent then.

"Aren't you going to ask me what I did mean?" she asked finally.

Duane laughed softly.

"I was just hoping you'd tell me without asking," he said.

She did turn and look at him then. In the dusk her face made an ivory oval.

"That's what I meant," she said. "Part of you I can understand just like I knew you'd say that before you did. The rest of you is harder to see into than a chunk of flint."

"What do you think you see?" he asked in a friendly voice.

"I see a man," she said. "Not like a braggart or a fool but a riding man. I see eyes that mask a thinking man. I see two guns tied down in a very special way."

"Did your husband wear his guns like that?" Duane asked.

"My husband didn't tie down guns," she said. "He carried one gun, a musket, over his shoulder. We were children really when we married back in Tennessee and then he went away to war. My husband, Mr. Duane, left his bones in the mud at Bloody Shiloh Church when the Tennessee Infantry didn't quite push Grant into the river. The books all say it was a glorious battle and a great day for the South, but my husband never came home to me."

They stood silent for a long time.

"I've known other men," she said at last. It was both statement and invitation and required no immediate answer.

"You wear guns like a fighting man," Sally Burke said, "but you ride in town and eat at my table instead of Ace's place. You ride like a cattleman, but your hands aren't calloused from the rope. You wear boots of the finest leather I've ever seen, but there's no silver conchos on your saddle. Every way I look at you, Mr. Duane, you are and you aren't. It puzzles me."

"We're going to be friends," Buck Duane said. "In time I won't puzzle you any more."

"I wonder," she said. "I wonder if the woman lives who'll ever really know you like she could an ordinary man. I'll be glad to find out."

A bat went silently in and out of the

cottonwood branches, filling its belly with insects snapped on the wing.

"It's this town that bothers me," Duane said then. "What's wrong with this place, Sally?"

"So you sense it already," she said. "Try to find out for yourself, Buck. Then come and ask me again. I won't lie to you but I think it's better you form your own opinion first. You won't do that here under my big tree though."

"I know," Duane said. "I know. I'll go down to Ace Holden's place presently. That's where the action is. Everybody and everything in this town points to Ace Holden. I've been told that twice today."

"Isn't that your answer then?"

"I don't think so," Buck Duane said. "I'll get the idea all the fingers point to Ace Holden because it's the easy thing to do. I haven't seen Ace yet, but I wonder what I'll find when I do. Will he really be man enough for everybody to be afraid of? What's what I wonder."

"Don't wonder aloud to anybody but me," she said. "Maybe it isn't even safe to talk to me. That bat might be listening. You're a smart man, Mr. Buck Duane, and now I wonder something else. I wonder if you're as good with those guns as you are with wondering."

"I try to be," he said.

"It seems to me I've heard you were," she said. "I've heard of a Duane. I don't know where or when. It isn't important anyway. You and I are friends."

Sally Burke turned to face him, and on a sudden impulse they shook hands there in the dusk. Her hand was soft and warm, but her grip was steady like a man's.

Buck Duane went back in the house and belted on his guns. He spun the cylinders and settled them in the holsters exactly to his taste. It was a warm evening so he left his long-tailed coat in the room and wore only a vest over a clean white shirt. He took off the rider's neckerchief he wore by day and left the shirt open at the throat. From that moment on at least one of his hands was never more than inches from the butt of a holstered Colt.

Buck Duane was a fighting man with those guns. He'd shot the head of a striking rattler in a draw that was already one of the legends of the West. He lived by the things his gunman father had taught him as a boy.

"Don't ever wear a gun unless you're willing to use it," the elder Duane had said.

"Don't touch it till you start to draw."

"When you draw a gun kill your man. Don't ever bluff a man, boy. Kill him or let him be."

Whenever he prepared for a possible fight Duane could hear his father's voice again, just as clear as if the man were there in the room and he was just a boy again.

The father had killed by choice. Buck Duane never did. His worst nightmare was the remembered face of the first man he'd had to kill. That first shooting was in self defense, and so were all the others. The gunsels who feared Duane would never have dreamed it of course, but he hated to kill. He always felt sick, body and soul, after a shoot-out.

It was only a half mile from Sally Burke's boarding house to Ace Holden's place, but Buck Duane wouldn't have dreamed of walking the distance. His pack horse was still at the Livery Stable, but Bullet was in the pasture back of Sally's barn. He came to Duane's call and let himself be saddled.

It wasn't only that no Texan would willingly walk across the street if he could ride. Depending on what happened in the saloon, Duane might have to ride for his life.

A horse half a mile away wouldn't have been much use to him then.

The front of the saloon was a blaze of light that spilled out across the street. Buck Duane could see men going in and out. As he came closer he could hear the mixed and compounded blast of sound that always came from these places when there was a crowd. Mixed into the other noises he could hear a piano and a fiddle being played.

Duane tied Bullet at the near end of the hitching rail and stepped up on the wooden walkway fronting the gambling hall. He noticed that the windows fronting the place had been painted over with whitewash. Light spilled through, but no one on the sidewalk as he was could see inside except by going right up to the door. It was a common practice with bars where the patrons were likely to be men on the run. They didn't have to worry so much about who might be at their backs.

Buck Duane pushed right through the swinging doors without hesitation but managed to sweep the barroom with a quick glance before he got far inside. To his relief there was no one in the room who he could recognize from the outlaw years. Recognition was a risk he took on every job he undertook for Captain MacNelly and the Rangers.

The room wasn't crowded. It was only a Thursday night, and the big play would wait until Saturday in a town as small as this one. There were a dozen men and half a dozen women at the bar. They seemed to be trying to make up for their small number by the amount of noise they could make.

A couple of the men looked like merchants. Most of the rest were riders from nearby ranches. Off by themselves were three men whom Buck Duane spotted instantly for professional gun-hands.

There was a poker table going at one end of the room and five men seated there playing strict attention to their cards. Only one of them really caught Duane's attention. He was tall and slender, not skinny but gracefully lean. His age could have been anything from forty-five to sixty, but was probably about halfway between. His black hair was beginning to thin and show streaks of grey. He wore a grey frock coat and trousers, expensive boots, and a spotless white linen shirt. There was a diamond ring on the third finger of his right hand a very heavy gold watch chain across his vest.

Ordinarily Duane would have pegged the

man as a gambler, but somehow this one didn't fit the role. The hand which held his cards carelessly over the table was sunbrowned as a professional gambler's never is. His face was tanned also, but it was the face of an educated and cultivated man of the world. His lips smiled easily as he said something to the other players, but Duane had an instant realization that this could be a very dangerous man. If he was armed, the weapons were concealed by his long coat.

As Duane came into the room this man raised his head and for an instant looked right at the Ranger. It was just a glance but Buck Duane felt as if he'd been examined, classified, and stored in the man's memory file.

"Eyes like that," he thought, "could look right through and count the joints in my backbone."

The feeling of uneasiness was so strong, that he almost, but not quite broke step and turned to face the man. He managed to control himself and walked on to the bar.

"I'd like to talk to Ace," he told the bartender after he'd ordered a beer.

"It don't work quite that way," the man said with a trace of insolence that hadn't showed in his manner earlier in the day. "If

Ace wants to talk to you, he sends for you. Did he send for you mister?"

Duane fixed the bartender with a cold grey eye.

"You tell him it's Buck Duane," he said. "When you say it, it's Mister Duane. You tell him I want to talk business."

The barkeep didn't like the look or the tone, but he still hesitated. Duane's left hand shot out and caught the man's shirt front above the apron he wore. He yanked the fellow forward with enough force so his fat paunch slammed against the bar and the wind was jolted out of him.

"Tell Ace," he said. "Now."

His arm straightened and shoved the man back against the counter under the mirror. A couple of bottles tottered to the floor and smashed. The man didn't even wait to clean up the mess. He crab-walked along behind the bar, keeping his face turned to Duane, until he came to a door at the end of the mirror and bolted through.

Buck Duane didn't turn his head, but the mirror showed him that the men and women at the bar had seen the byplay and were watching him out of the corner of their eyes. The three gunsels off to his left pushed back their chairs and stood up, but made no move to come closer to him. Only the poker players seemed totally wrapped up in their game.

The bartender came out of the door again. Ace Holden was with him.

Holden was a big man, maybe six-foot-two or three in his tooled leather boots, and broad across the shoulders. He was heavy with the fat of good living and had a paunch that bulged out over his gunbelt. The holster was empty. There were rings with flashing red and green stones on both hands, and diamond buttons to his vest. His face was red and sweat had stained his shirt and the armholes of his black frock coat. The eyes looking out of the beefy face were small and mean and vicious.

"You Duane?" he asked needlessly. "What makes you think I want to talk business this time of night?"

"Whenever I try to talk it with anyone else around here," Duane said, "somehow or other your name comes up. Seems to me if I'm going to talk at all, it'd have to be with you."

"Well now," Holden said expansively. "Well now, that might or mightn't be the case. All depends on what sort of business

40

you got in mind. Ain't plannin' on opening another saloon, are you?"

"Not that," Duane said.

"Well then, come on and let's go back and set where we can talk."

Instead of taking Duane through the door which presumably led to his office Holden led the way to a table far enough from the bar itself so they couldn't be overheard. He took the chair that put his back to the wall. That left Duane to sit with his back to the three gunslingers.

Duane wasn't buying. He picked the chair up and moved it so that he faced the room also and sat beside Ace Holden instead of across the table.

"You're mighty careful for a business man," Holden said.

Buck Duane said nothing.

"I'm a mite careful too," Ace Holden continued. "Way we are now neither of us could put a gun on the other 'thout my friends seeing it."

"You're too careful," Duane said. "I'm not riding gun hand. Not this trip. I heard tell this was good sweetwater country, and I came to see about starting a spread here myself. Nothing raunchy about it. I got money to pay in a draft on a San Antone

41

bank. All fair and square."

"That ain't the point," Ace Holden said. "You only been here less'n a day now. Suppose there was land to sell, and suppose – just suppose – I might mebbe influence the seller to make you a deal, how do we know you be the sort of man to fit into our community here? You come riding in with tied down guns and your head in the air lke you was Frank Younger or Jesse James hisself. This here's a peaceful town. Everybody sort of makes it a point to get along."

"I'm a peaceful man," Duane said. "I don't push anybody. What's that got to do with ranching?"

"It ain't so much the ranching it's got to do with. Round here let's just say it's to do with the living." He threw back his head and roard with laughter. One of his big hands slapped the table twice, palm down.

Buck Duane saw that the gunmen were watching. He took the table slapping for a signal of some sort to them, but they didn't move.

"All right, Mr. Holden," he said. "It ain't all that funny. I figure to go on living, here or any place. You ain't answered my question about land to sell."

"I ain't made up my mind yet," Holden said.

"I suppose there's government land for the homesteading?" Duane said. His inference was plain enough. He could buy direct.

Ace Holden went on laughing but the mean little eyes narrowed. There wasn't any humor in his expression when he spoke again.

"You're a stranger here," he said, "and that there idea just proves it for sure. There's homestead land all right, but it ain't healthy land. Them as gets it is short of water, short of feed, short of supplies. You might even say they was short of time. Yessiree, that's about it. Them homesteaders is short-lived people."

"So, if I want land, I wait for you to make up your mind," Duane said. "No offense meant. Like you say I'm a stranger in these parts."

"Now you're seeing the light," Ace Holden said. "That's just about right. You wait for me to make up my mind about how you fit into our homey little community. When I make it up, I'll let you know one way or t'other. Meantimes, if you get impatient, a man's always free to ride out the way he rode in."

Holden got to his feet and so did Duane. Ace Holden made no effort to shake hands. He turned and walked back towards the bar. As he did, one of the thin-faced gunmen stepped out to talk to him.

Ace Holden stopped walking. His back was to Buck Duane and his broad shoulders and massive body hid the gunman from sight. The way the two of them stood a clump of bar patrons kept them from being reflected in the mirror.

Buck Duane felt the old familiar icy knot of tension form in the pit of his stomach. It was always that way just before he had to fight for his life. He never wanted to kill, but he knew the time had come again. His fingers hung close to the butt of the heavy black forty-five.

When the action came it was lightning fast.

Ace Holden took two fast steps to his own right. It took him out of the line of fire and exposed the man who had been hidden from Duane's line of sight.

The gunman had no delusions about chivalry. Like all his kind he murdered for cash and never gave his victim a chance when it could be helped. His gun was already out when Holden stepped aside, and his left hand was sweeping down and in to fan the hammer for a burst.

Buck Duane went down on his right knee and his own gun seemed almost to jump out of the holster into his hand. With the perfect timing achieved by years of endless practice his thumb cocked the hammer as the muzzle came up and his trigger finger tightened so that the shot crashed exactly as the weapon came level. He aimed his whole body rather than just the gun. The whole thing was so fast that no spectator managed to follow it.

The wiry gunman was fast. He got off his first shot so that it merged with the report of Duane's gun. The trouble with fanning, though, was that it was never aimed fire. The fanner relied on a quick burst to bracket and flatten his man.

This one had no time for a burst. His first shot went over Duane's shoulder where the Ranger had dropped to his knee. Then Duane's shot took him and killed him.

That the man got off a second shot at all was a tribute to his speed. It was instinct or reflex or the paralyzing shock of the forty-five slug that moved his hand. He was dead on his feet when the hammer fell.

It was pure accident, but the bullet hit Duane's left arm just below the shoulder. If it had struck bone, he would have been crippled for life. As it was, the shock of the ragged flesh wound swung him partly around, twisting his body to the left, and temporarily putting that arm out of commission.

Only a powerful man with a will of iron could have kept himself under control. Buck Duane managed it. The smoking muzzle of his big Colts swung back to cover Holden and his two other gun hands. The gunsels made no move at all.

Ace Holden put his hands up shoulder high.

"I ain't armed," he yelled. "Everybody witness! I got no gun. He'll murder me."

"Somebody give him a gun," Duane said. His voice was pitched low, but in the sudden silence that followed the crashing shots it carried to all parts of the room.

Blood was soaking Duane's shirt sleeve and dripping from the hanging fingers of his left hand, but the big Ranger didn't seem to notice. His eyes were icy cold and the hand holding his gun never wavered.

"Give him a gun," he said again.

"For God's sake no!" Ace Holden yelled.

"I got no quarrel with you, Duane. It was Sam's idea. He thought he knew you from some place. I swear it. I won't fight you."

Buck Duane knew perfectly well that if their roles had been reversed Ace Holden would have shot him dead in his tracks. He knew that the big man would never forgive him for the humiliation of having had to beg for his life. As long as Ace Holden lived he, Buck Duane, could expect a bullet in the back the first moment his guard was relaxed in the slightest.

Holden's man would never have fired on him without orders. Every man and woman in the room knew it.

Even so, Duane couldn't bring himself to pull trigger on an unarmed man who kept his hands up. To his last day he'd never know why, but Buck Duane had never killed except in self defense. He hated taking the life of another man. Once attacked, he could be a smoothly coordinated, lightning fast killing machine, but he could not or would not kill except to preserve his own life.

After a moment he dropped his gun back in its holster.

Chapter V

There was a long sigh of relief from the people in the bar. Then the silence was broken by an entirely new voice from the doorway which led into the hotel lobby.

"If you'd murdered him, Mister, I'd have had to shoot you down. I'm glad you didn't, because I'd have hated to do it."

It was a woman's voice, calm and collected and with the crisp accent and cultivated tone of an educated lady. As Buck Duane turned slowly he saw her in the doorway.

She stood straight and proud, although actually she was a small woman and lightly boned. For all of that she held the ivory handled derringer steady as a rock. She wore a dress of powder blue material with a skirt divided for riding like a man and soft leather boots showing under the trailing edge. Her eyes were black and her hair raven-wing dark and curling about a beautiful oval face. To Duane's eye she could have been any age, but of a surety she was all woman.

He recovered himself. "Why thank you, Miss. I'm glad too that you didn't shoot."

She made a simple gesture and the derringer vanished into a pocket of the dress.

"All's well that ends well," she said in a lighter tone. "Now, sir, it's time something was done about that wound of yours. You're bleeding on the floor." She raised her voice: "Dan, get your bag."

"Yes, my dear." It was the distinguished looking man at the poker table who answered. He reached down to the floor beside his chair and straightened up holding a black leather doctor's bag with heavy Mexican silver fittings.

"Come over here, man," he said easily. "I'll put a ligature around that arm for now, and then we'll all go and get the wound properly dressed."

"I'll be obliged," Duane said. "No man can make blood as fast as it runs out." He walked over to the table and sat down.

"Something of a philosopher as well?" the doctor said. "Good man. This won't take a minute."

He deftly slit the sleeve of Duane's shirt to expose the wound, applied a wad of cotton and gauze and twisted a tourniquet above the cut so that the bleeding stopped.

"That should do it for now," he said. "We'll go on to my office for a real dressing. You can ride, I think?"

"I can ride," the Ranger said. He thought of many rides for life he'd made with wounds far worse than this. "But first I'll buy the house a drink."

Ace Holden had vanished into his office and his two remaining gunmen with him. A couple of swampers had carried out the dead man and thrown sand to cover the pool of blood on the floor. Now the customers crowded up to the bar.

Buck Duane poured himself a good four fingers from the whiskey bottle that was brought to the table and drank it down all at once. The burning warmth of the raw spirits began to melt the cold knot in his stomach.

Buck Duane, the doctor and the small woman rode out of town up the hill to where the big houses of the well-to-do stood under the shade of live oak and cottonwood trees. It was only about a mile to go.

The doctor and his sister Ann – he'd introduced himself as Daniel Mills – lived in the biggest house of all. There was a butler to meet them at the door and a scurry of

Mexican maids to take their hats and bring drinks.

The doctor's office was in the ground floor rear, and he took Duane there at once for a highly professional cleaning and dressing of the wound. Duane noticed that he washed his hands and instruments in liquid from a big jug of grain alcohol before starting to work on the wound.

"A newfangled notion," Doctor Mills said wryly. "Read about it in a journal from the University at Edinburgh in Scotland. Some of my colleagues laugh at it, but I get many fewer infected wounds since I began its use."

Mills cleaned Duane's wound carefully and bound it up.

"Should be right as rain in a few days for a healthy chap like yourself," he said. "You're lucky the bone wasn't even nicked. Clean wound is always best, I say."

They went back into the big front parlor where Ann Mills was waiting for them, and the servants had brought cold meat and cakes and wine.

"Sit down and rest a bit," Ann said. "It's late, but there's still time to talk. Why on earth did that man ever draw on you, Mr.

Duane? Had he really known you somewhere else?"

"Not to my knowledge, Miss Mills," Duane said, and helped himself to food and drink. "I think he drew because Ace Holden told him to."

"I think so too," the doctore said, "but why would Ace do that? Had you just quarreled with him? I saw you talking."

"It puzzles me," Duane said. "No, we didn't quarrel. I'd just told him I was thinking of buying a ranch in this beautiful valley. For some reason or other he didn't seem to like the idea, but there wasn't any actual quarrel. Certainly nothing was said that I'd have thought worth killing a man for."

"Did you defy Ace?" Ann asked. "He's a most arbitrary man and used to lording it over the people here. If his temper was bad tonight anyway, he might take offense where another man wouldn't."

"No," Duane said. "Not even defiance, though I might have done just that had the talk gone on much further. That isn't all that puzzles me either, ma'am. What makes everybody around here so afraid of Ace Holden?"

"I'm not afraid of him," she said with spirit.

"I believe you aren't," Duane said. "That isn't what I meant. But in just one day I've talked to other folk who were. If I wanted to buy land, they say, I must see Ace. I never heard of a set-up like this any place in Texas before. Does he own this town, or what?"

"Not exactly own," the doctor said. "No, you couldn't really say he owns High Valley. Not in the sense of bought and paid for anyway."

"In another sense you might say he did," Ann Mills said. "It is sort of an unusual thing for Texas. He has a mortgage on the valley. That mortgage is fear."

"What Ann means," her brother said, "is you aren't the first man around here Ace Holden took a dislike to who's had to fight for his life. I'll admit though that you're the first of the lot to come out of the fight alive. Those boys of Ace's don't usually miss."

"That one didn't exactly miss," Duane said. "He was just a mite slower than he should have been. It's an edge the gun fanner ought never to give the other man. Because he don't aim, he's got to be a lot quicker getting the shots off."

"Ahem," mills chucked and then said,

"For Sam that's only an academic point by now. The question remains, just what are you going to do, Mr. Duane? You don't seem to share the general fear of Ace and his boys."

"I just reckon to take care of myself," Duane said. "If the other fellow starts a ruckus, I finish it."

"So you do – and most effectively, I must say. By the way, if it's any help to you, Sam Huie was the fastest of those three."

"That's right," Ann added. "Since you took Sam, you could take the other two as long as they stand up to you like he did."

"Or they could backshoot me, you mean. That's been tried before, Miss Mills. I'm a Texan and so I'm a stubborn and independent man. I can take care of myself."

"Seems to me someone else around here used to say that," the doctor said over his wine glass. "It was Bill Bass, if I remember rightly."

There was meaning behind the remark which Duane couldn't fathom. It wasn't quite a threat, nor yet a question. More like a test thrown out to see how he'd react.

Duane decided to appear perfectly open and candid. "Bass? That's the feller whose papers I brought back with me from San Antone. Got himself killed down there, and they figured at the Bank since I was coming right up here anyway it'd be faster than the mail." He stopped and laughed. "Maybe save postage too, I guess."

Neither of his hearers seemed overly surprised.

"You weren't by chance there when he was killed?" Doctor Mills asked. "No last words for his widow or anything like that?"

"Not that I know of," Duane said. "Nobody said anything about his living long enough to talk, and I wasn't there myself."

"Oh yes, of course." There was a sudden feeling of relaxed tension in the room.

Buck Duane didn't like it. Somehow they'd been hanging on the answer to that one question. What did they think he'd say? More to the point, was it something they were afraid they'd hear? He decided he needed to know a lot more about this couple.

"I'm most grateful to you both," he said, getting to his feet, "but it's been a right long day. What with loss of blood and all, I'd best be on my way."

They urged him to spend the night, but he refused. The doctor laughed at the idea of payment for dressing the wound.

"Just watching that marvelous draw of yours was payment enough," he protested. "I really didn't do anything."

Buck Duane watched the shadows as he rode back to Sally Burke's place, but there were no threats or lurking figures. He put Bullet in the barn, and walked up to the house and to his room. Nobody else was up and about.

Duane was asleep almost as soon as he hit the bed. That is most of him slept. One tiny corner of his mind listened for any unusual sound or presence. A man who's been hunted for years can never really sleep as sound as other men. His life has for too long depended upon unending alertness to any variant from the norm. Had anyone even come close to the window, Duane would have been instantly awake and reaching for his gun without any conscious awareness of what had roused him.

That was what happened in the morning. He woke – became totally awake, and gun in hand – all in an instant. Without knowing how he knew, he was aware of someone standing in the hall outside his door.

He was right. There was a soft tap on the door and then Sally's voice: "Are you all right, Buck? Don't get up unless you feel like it. I heard about last night. But if you're hungry, I've saved some breakfast and the rest have gone out."

"I'll be with you in a minute," he called back. "Thanks a lot."

Sally Burke gave him a big platter of bacon and fried eggs, biscuits and hone, fried potatoes and a slab of left-over canned peach pie with a lighter crust than the best San Antonio chef had ever made. He ate heartily and then they sat with china mugs of hot boiled coffee so thick the spoon would almost stand erect.

It was only then that she tried to talk.

"They tell me you shot Sam Huie last night, Buck. Does that mean you got the answer to your questions?"

"Not exactly," Duane said, "I met Ace Holden and we didn't like each other worth shucks. It wasn't enough for him to tell me to get out of town. He had to tell his man to help me on my way. If you heard the story, you know it was no stand-up fight. More like backshooting me, except that Sam wasn't quite as good as he thought he was.

"When that was over I met Doctor Mills and his sister and they took me home for wine and to tell me in their own way to get out of town. They weren't quite as blunt

57

about it as Ace had been, but in the end it all added up to the same thing. Every living soul I've seen in High Valley wants me gone except you, Sally."

"Since you're stubborn enough to stay around anyway," she said, "I might as well tell you what I can. This High Valley range is a rather special type of place. We're more or less cut off from the rest of the state up here. It's wonderful grazing land and the river gives plenty of water, but it's only been settled about ten years. We're out ahead of most people and the real law hasn't caught up with us yet.

"That makes a perfect set-up for somebody like Ace Holden. As far as this valley is concerned he just took over as the law."

"How could he do that?"

"He did it because he made everybody afraid of him," she said. "Right at first a couple of ranchers told him where to go when he started pushing them around. I can show you their neat wooden crosses in the graveyard back of the church."

"As raw as that?" Buck Duane asked.

"Not quite." Sally poured him more coffee. "Ace didn't shoot anybody himself that we know of. One of the men got into a fight with his gun hands over cards. The other was found bushwhacked with Winchester slugs in his back. Then there was Willis Tremacher, who has the big hardware store in town. He was all for getting up a citizens' committee and hiring a marshal. Right then was when two wagon loads of goods he'd ordered and paid for were raided by bandits. The drivers were killed."

"I see," Duane said quietly. "Now nobody else wants to be first to stand on the spot marked X. That's all very fine, but isn't it dangerous for Ace too? Suppose somebody hired a killer to take him out of the picture? Or suppose I'd shot him last night like maybe I ought to have when he was under my gun? Wouldn't that solve the problem all in one neat little package?"

She gave a short, bitter laugh. "Oh, don't fool yourself that hasn't been thought of. It has. More than once. Only I guess whoever's back of all the trouble must have thought of it first. You see Ace doesn't claim to give orders in his own name. He claims to be acting for somebody else, that the killings are ordered by somebody else."

"Who?" Buck Duane felt he was hitting paydirt now.

Sally shook her head. "That's the devil of it. Nobody knows. The only name used is Mr. Smith. Mr. Smith wants this. Mr. Smith has so-and-so killed. Only nobody ever saw Mr. Smith. There's all sorts of yarns. He's Reeder the Renegade. He's one of the Youngers. He's a Mexican hidalgo with connections this side of the border. The story that makes most sense to me is he has an outlaw and rustler stronghold somewhere West of here in the hills back of the Rainbow Ranch – that's the big spread at the head of the valley. Only thing wrong with that theory is he never rustles steers in here. His men aren't seen. Somebody gets killed, that's all, and Ace Holden issues orders."

"What kind of orders?" Duane asked. "Surely that ought to indicate something?"

"See what you can make of it then. Of course I don't know the whole story. For one thing anybody borrows money here gets it from the High Valley Bank. The owner on record of that bank is Ace Holden. Anybody wants a loan gets one, with lots of fine print in the papers he signs. So everybody owes Ace, and back of Ace is this Mr. Smith. Only rancher around here dared bank outside was Bill Bass, and don't think folks aren't saying that's why he's dead.

"Ranchers have to buy their stock from Ace Holden, on credit with easy terms and high interest. Where does Ace get the beef critters to sell? They're driven down from the Rainbow. Some of them are Spanish cattle, which is where the Mexican hidalgo story got started. Nobody knows. They're good steers and this range makes them better, but everybody's in debt to Ace and whoever backs Ace. Then when they sell the cattle it has to be to Ace. The Rainbow hands drive all stock out of here to the market in one big herd. The men know they could get a better price if they made their own drives to railhead, but they just don't dare."

"I can see one thing plain enough," Duane said. "This Smith hombre, whoever he is, can take over the valley for his personal ranch any time he wants. All he has to do is foreclose all the notes and mortgages people signed at a time when he's already fixed it so they can't pay, like refusing to buy their cattle. Meantime, he's got everybody stocking range and making improvements at their own expense while he sits back and skims the cream. Sooner or later he'll grab the whole cow, if he isn't stopped."

"Can't the law stop him, Buck?" she

asked suddenly. "Oh, I don't mean that drunken fool Judge Gowanus. I mean Texas law. Why can't somebody like you ride out of here and report all this to the Governor or the Rangers or somebody?"

"I could do that easy," Buck Duane said, "only I know just enough about the law to tell you it wouldn't do one bit of good. You can't arrest a man nobody ever saw and who maybe doesn't exist. Besides he hasn't done anything."

"Ace has," she said. "Why don't they arrest Ace?"

"Because they wouldn't have any proof he done one thing that was criminal. That's why not," Duane said. "It's no crime to have people scared of you. Outslickering the borrower with fine print in a loan paper's not criminal either. The law says a man's supposed to know what he signs. And if all the cattlemen sell to the same person, there ain't a law on the books that makes a criminal of that buyer. He's just a smart business man.

"Now it would be different, let's say, if somebody came forth with some legal evidence that could stand up in a court of law. Say there was a witness with proof who did the bushwhacking, or somebody could produce a threat to his life in writing. It might even do if a couple of ranchers would stand up and swear they were made to sell their cattle under pain of death. You reckon any of them might do that?"

"You know better," Sally said. "You know darn good and well they wouldn't dare."

"That sort of makes it a Mexican stand-off," Duane said. "Seems a shame too. Specially since it must be exactly what this Smith feller must have figured on right from the first. Of course there's just one other thing. The folks here might all get together and run Ace out or kill him if they had to, fight off this Smith and his gang if they came, sell their cattle for top prices and some way pay off those loans. Course it wouldn't be easy, any of it."

"Some folks have been nigh desperate enough to try against any odds," Sally said, "except for one thing I didn't mention, because I can hardly believe it myself, let alone repeat it to a stranger like you.

"This Mr. Smith, he has an ace in the hole nobody could fight, even if they knew for sure what it was."

"Tell me," Duane said. "Maybe it might help."

"Well, promise me now you won't just say I've gone clean out of my wits.

"The word is that, if Mr. Smith is crossed, if he ever chooses, he can kill the river."

"Kill the river?" Duane said. "High Valley River? Now how in the name of all that's holy does anybody kill a river?

"A river's a thing of nature like a mountain. Like the sun or a rainstorm."

"I don't know," she said. "If anybody's been told how, they haven't passed it on to me. All I know is that the ranchers believe he can do what he says. He's done everything else he said, hasn't he? Bill Bass sort of hinted he'd talk in San Antonio, and Bill's dead. Ten to one somebody from Ace followed and shot him down. And without the river this valley couldn't be worth a wooden nutmeg to anything bigger'n jackrabbits.

"Save for Stover's well down south of here it's the only sweet water for sixty-seventy miles in any direction. Cattle need water, and folks are no different than their cow critters. Truth is, nobody dares take a chance Smith is right. That's just exactly how buffaloed he's got them all."

"He hasn't got me scared," Duane said. "Not yet he hasn't anyhow."

"What can you do?" Sally asked. "If all the other folks can't do anything, what makes you think you can? Just one man and all? How can you?"

"I'm not the rest of your folks," the Ranger said. "I'm Buck Duane and I don't like being pushed around by man or ghost or anybody hides behind the name of Smith. The first thing I'll do is go look at this river of yours. If it can be killed I'll find out. I figure I'll see it fast as this Smith could. Anyway, when I get back you'll know about the river and if there's a gang holed up in the hills."

"You'd really do that?"

"Sure I would. It'll take me out of town for a few days till this arm heals anyway. Time I get back I'll likely need two hands to shoot with."

Chapter VI

Buck Duane saddled Bullet and got his pack horse from the livery stable, loaded all his gear, and went by the saloon. The bartender wasn't happy to see him, but he put up a beer. Duane drank it down and said nothing.

"You leaving town?" the bartender asked.

"What else you think I loaded my stuff for?" Duane said in a surly tone. He wanted it assumed he was giving up and moving on for good. "I'm riding out aways, but that don't mean I won't be back."

"Sure," the bartender said and wiped the bar. His expression was scornful. "Sure, fella. Anything you say."

I fooled that one, Duane thought as he mounted up. Maybe even Ace will believe him. He'll want to because he can claim he scared me out. Make up a little for the way he had to crawl last night. He'll want to think I'm running.

This Mr. Smith now – if there really is a

66

Mr. Smith – he might not be fooled so easy. He's got to be smarter than Ace Holden, or Ace wouldn't work for him. It'd be the other way around. He'll be worried about me after last night, and he'll likely try to think of what he'd do if he was me. Once he figures out I wouldn't likely just up and run, the rest of it'll come to him fast enough.

Duane remembered something Captain MacNelly used to tell his men.

"If you can out-think the man you're after," the veteran Ranger officer would say, "you've got him. Sooner or later you've got him. Sometimes you come up against one you can't out-think, and when you do, outrun him. Keep just a jump ahead of where he's sure you are. Then you'll have him too before it's over."

One of the Confederate cavalry commanders in the late war had said much the same thing. "Get thar fustest with the mostest."

This was a case where Buck Duane knew he'd have to do just that. If there really was an outlaw gang in the hills, and they caught him in the open, it was all up with Buck Duane. He'd been an outlaw himself for enough years to have a proper respect for the fighting ability of the owlhoot fraternity.

They had to be either good with their guns or dead. On their own ground and against a single man they were very, very good indeed.

Duane had to move fast and far. Swing a wide loop, as the ranchers would say.

He headed out of the valley to begin with, then swung away from the river and the road which bordered it. He'd rather have waited for nightfall, but had a persistent feeling that speed was of the greatest importance.

Heading back up the valley, he stayed almost in the shadow of the western hills. That meant he couldn't be seen by anyone in or near the town even if they used a powerful telescope. The valley was anywhere from twenty to thirty miles broad throughout most of its length, only narrowing where the river came out of the hills. It was roughly forty miles in length.

It was a real prize that Mr. Smith was grasping for, Buck Duane thought as he rode and looked about him. It was a kingdom in miniature, richer and fairer than many a European or Asiatic principality.

To an outland visitor the grasslands would have been as monotonous as a placid sea except that the color was green or splashed with the hues of grass flowers in season. In places the waving tips reached saddle-high on a mounted man, particularly where, as in High Valley, there was water and sun to spare.

Within the grass plains themselves there is endless, merciless warfare between species. Grasses are long-lived, can reproduce by seed or root, and are all equally at home on the prairies. The different sorts struggle without cease for light and water and nutrients.

The root systems of different grasses grow at varying levels in the soil. Each species, as it tries to expand, must battle with the others. Sometimes a minor factor makes the different between success and failure. Big bluestem flourishes on the fat soils of the moist lower slopes such as the ground where Duane rode.

The little bluestem, only half the height of its cousin grass, becomes dominant as the slopes increase. Its root system is more efficient at gathering and storing water, and that gives it a real advantage on the higher plains.

The true prairie is a mixture of living plants whose roots go down to different levels, some shallow, some probing many feet into the soil. Together they bind the earth in a carpet so thick and tough and hard that again and again the iron plows of the homesteaders broke before they could turn a furrow.

Violet, ground plum, wood sorrel and cat's paw flower in early spring and then lie shaded by the summer grass. Other flowers like the hawkweed stake out their claim by growing a tight rosette of leaves to shade the soil. As the grasses grow higher the hawkweed's stem grows with them to keep its crowning rosette in the sun.

Through all of these plants and more Duane rode north and west. Under the cover of wavering grasses, the rodents and birds and insects at home in the grass hurried to get out of his path. The fragrance of sun on grass, spiced by the cool wind off the hills tingled his nostrils and freshened his blood like a strange and wonderful wine.

Far in the distance lay the silver ribbon of High Valley River, fringed by live oak and cottonwood. Where it widened into placid pools the westering sun struck blinding corruscations of reflected light.

Most of the ranch houses he saw were near the river and the road. He stayed well back of them so as to attract no attention that could be avoided. He couldn't be sure of course that some rider wouldn't see him at a distance, but he hoped that no thought would be given to his passing, particularly if he was too far off to be recognized.

He camped in the grass that night and ate cold food that Sally Burke had packed into his saddle bags. It was cold after the heat of the day, but he risked not even the smallest fire. Piled grasses made his bed, and it was far softer than – any that Duane had known in the years gone by.

Soon after starting out in the morning Duane came to a place where the valley narrowed to only about five miles in width and the hills steepened and straightened to a wall. Above this point the hills fell back again and the slopes decreased, but this narrow gap marked the commencement of the Rainbow Ranch. To make double sure, the whole gap had been fenced across with the new and expensive barbed wire just now beginning to be imported from Chicago, St. Louis and Kansas City.

Like most riders of the open range Buck Duane hated and despised the wire as a cruel and inhuman trap for beasts of all sorts. On this particular morning he disliked it even more than usual.

Its presence meant that he'd have to get

out of the valley in order to continue in the direction he wanted to go. It was too high for Bullet, let alone the burdened pack horse, to have jumped.

He carried wire cutters in his bags as a matter of course, and could have made a breach in a minute's time. The trouble was that, even if he tried to twist the cut ends of the wire together the first line rider along the fence would have known someone had gone through. If Ace's people were looking for him that would give them a hot trail to follow. Accordingly he pushed off to the left, where a notch cut into the low bluff on his side of the fence.

About a mile from the notch natural caution, strengthened by long years on the run, halted him. He got a pair of powerful army-type field glasses out of his saddle bags and carefully inspected the ground ahead. Nothing unusual showed. The grassy hills rose in easy swells on both sides of the notch, growing steeper and steeper as the land rose away from the prairie. There were no rock piles behind which a bushwacker could hide and no trees. The fast growing, deep rooted grasses preempted all water and ground which might have nourished larger growth.

Buck Duane decided it was safe to use the

pass, but he never for an instant relaxed his alertness as he rode in.

It was well that he did not. The two men had lain in ambush in the tall grass back of a slight hollow on the side of the nearest hill. They'd taken the trouble to throw and hobble their horses back of the crown of the hill.

Nothing at all showed except waving grass till the men got partly upright and prepared to aim their Winchesters. That made a wrong ripple in the even flow of grass before the wind.

Duane couldn't see into the grass, but the wrongness triggered him to instant action. He was over the far side of Bullet, hanging on by saddle horn and stirrup like an Indian, and pounding his mount in a dead run around the flank of the hill on the other side of the notch. He dropped the rein of the packhorse, but that animal, lightly loaded and actually brought as a spare mount in case of a long endurance chase, sensed anger and came racing at Bullet's heels.

Duane actually widened the gap by fifty yards before the first shot crashed out. The bushwackers, like most saddle men, were far more used to pistol than to rifle. The man-high grass made it hard to aim and the sudden dash of their intended victim threw them off balance.

At least a dozen shots were fired before Duane got out of effective range of the black-powder rifles. Only one came close and that nicked the pack horse's ear and sent him into a frenzied gallop.

Duane pulled Bullet to a halt. He considered going back and trying to capture and question one of the men, but decided against it when he saw them mount in haste and ride back towards the Rainbow spread.

That was Mr. Smith, he thought to himself. Maybe he had somebody posted to see if he'd really left the valley. Maybe he just played a hunch. He knew Duane was a stranger here, who'd come to the fence and decided not to cut it. That notch was a natural trap to toll a rider in, so he put his killers there. Ace Holden wasn't that smart. Not by a country mile he wasn't.

Again, he remembered Captain MacNelly's voice: "If you can't outthink them, you've got out-run 'em."

Duane pushed rapidly into the hills, but avoided making the wide, sweeping arc to avoid passing near Rainbow Range that the ordinary man would have done.

They wouldn't expect him to stay close, so

they'd run fast into the hills, expecting to cut his trail five or ten miles back in. Likely enough they'd miss his track completely, what with being in a hurry and not looking for it so close. Ordinarily rustlers and gunmen weren't much good at tracking anything smaller than a herd of steers.

His experience as a lone outlaw who often had to hunt and kill wild game for food had taught Buck Duane the art of tracking and a supreme contempt for those who had never learned.

He kept just off the skyline back of the first low ridge of hills bordering the valley. At regular intervals he'd dismount, go to the ridge and glass the area. He not only wanted to spot pursuit, but also to see and memorize the lay of the land back of that Rainbow fence.

He saw the two bushwackers riding hard up the river road to the cluster of ranch buildings. Once they reached it, however, no knot of riders came out and headed for the hills. He needn't worry about immediate pursuit.

Curiously enough that bothered him more than if he'd seen a posse on his track. Smith had been one jump ahead of him at the fence. What did he have up his sleeve now?

Except for the nature of his errand the Ranger would have been fascinated by the vista which stretched out before him. A line of green trees and sparkles of reflected sun marked High Valley River wind-up the middle of the valley. Stretching to the hlls on both sides was a sweep of tall grass like a green-gold sea, dotted by islands of feeding cattle. There were probably two or three thousand steers in sight, more than he'd expected to see by far.

If they were as thick further up, even a rich range like this one would be overgrazed. Where, he wondered, did they get such a herd, and what was the point of building it to unwieldy size?

There was only one logical answer. The Rainbow riders were either rustlers themselves or closely leagued to one of the big outlaw bands. The herds he saw were stolen, from the look of them, many from the big Mexican haciendas below the Rio Grande.

Anyone who knew the hills could drive them in a back entrance to the valley through the wild country running straight to the border. Once on the Rainbow range they could be fattened for another drive to market, and the brands doctored at leisure.

He'd been told that the valley ranchers bought Rainbow stock. Also other steers could be mixed into the one big market drive that went out of the valley each year. The big herd, all Rainbow owned but containing cattle with the varied brands of the small ranchers, made a perfect cover for disposal of the stolen stock.

Here was something that would certainly justify calling in MacNelly and a troop of Rangers to clear up the whole dirty situation in the Valley. Threats and unknown bushwackers were one thing. A major rustling headquarters with very probable international complications was something else again.

Buck Duane knew that he still had things to do before riding out of there however. He had to find an entrance by which the herds could be brought out of the hills onto Rainbow range. That should be easy enough.

He had also to determine if there were actually rustlers holed up in the hills and scout their hide-out so the Rangers would know how to take it. Actually Duane rather doubted if he'd find such a place. The Rainbow itself could offer safe and comfortable shelter to any number of riders as long as they came and went by the back door. There'd be no reason for the High Valley people to even suspect their presence.

Before making any drastic move Duane also needed to know what, if anything, was meant by the strange threat to 'kill the river.' He figured it was all a bluff but didn't quite dare to discount a man as smart as Mr. Smith had already shown himself to be. If there was a way to stop the water, there'd be no sense in attacking the ranch and having the whole valley ruined at the same time.

On the other hand, if Buck Duane could discover how the damage could be done, then the Rangers could think of a way to prevent it.

Last, but certainly not least of the tasks ahead, he had to learn the identity of Mr. Smith himself. He might be Ace Holden of course, or whoever ramrodded the Rainbow lying there in the distance. He might be the chief of an outlaw band, possibly Reeder the Renegade himself, or a business man a thousand miles off to the East who pulled the strings to make the valley people dance like marionettes. He might be anybody in the valley, maybe even a woman. Maybe Sally Burke herself. It was as tantalizing as trying to find the shadow of one tree in a wood on a moonless night.

Whoever he was he had a veritable gold mine in High Valley. He could use it as a safe base for rustling, storage of stolen or pillaged goods or hide-out for his men. He could make the people buy his steers and pay him interest on his loans. In time, when the march of settlement caught up to the valley and rustling would no longer be possible, he could take over the whole magnificent range for his own and make another fortune as an honest rancher. Stranger things had happened, and would again, in the incredibly rich Western country.

So far the only fly in this golden ointment, Buck Duane thought wryly, was himself. At the moment that was all he was, a minor inconvenience to be swatted and obliterated. That was the reason for the ambush. Later on, especially if Mr. Smith should realize Duane wasn't just a loan rancher looking for a spread but a Texas Ranger, the hunt would be on in earnest.

They'd know they had to kill him then. Every man and every gun at Mr. Smith's command would be mobilized to hunt him down. When that happened he knew he'd have to both outrun and outthink them all. Even then the odds against his getting safely back to the captain with his report would be long indeed.

He had to move now, and move fast while he still had a little leeway.

Duane rode back into the hills. He'd liked to have stayed and scouted the ranch buildings more closely, but he didn't dare take the time. Even at the distance he'd glassed the place from, he could see that it was a regular settlement, almost a village in itself.

The ranch house was big and rambling. There were outbuildings and sheds, barns, cookhouses, a smithy and bunkhouses as big as the barracks he'd seen at army posts. There were two big horse corrals and another where a few cattle were being held, probably waiting to have their stolen brands worked over.

The Ranger had decided on a long horseshoe loop through the hills that closed in the head of High Valley. He'd be sure to find the back way in.

He was lucky. It was barely four in the afternoon when he crossed what looked like a regular road leading towards the ranch. Thousands of cattle must have been driven this way over a long period of time to make such a beaten track.

Duane began to realize the size of the operation he was up against. This was no gang of outlaws and misfits, making hit-and-run cattle raids whenever they ran out of money. It was a big business, a very big business indeed. There'd have to be a big man back of it all. Somebody who had brains and money and talent and specialized knowledge to organize and then to keep things running smoothly.

For the first time Duane began to wonder if a single Ranger could possibly pit himself against such a set-up with any chance of coming out alive.

He didn't bother to follow the cattle trail into the point where it entered High Valley. That would be easy enough whenever the Rangers were ready to strike. Besides, if he followed it in he might run into guards or more bushwackers. There was no point in taking the risk.

He did ride onto the road as if he were going towards the valley, then turned his horses and backtracked for at least half a mile. Nobody in the area could have picked out his tracks in that trampled and hard-beaten strip.

Then he left the road where an outcropping of rock would hide his tracks and angled across country in search of a camping spot.

He had climbed high enough now so that the short upland grass was being challenged by clumps of trees, mostly the ubiquitous firs of the western uplands. He circled one such forest clump which covered a couple of acres of slope and found himself looking into the muzzle of an ancient Hawken buffalo rifle at a range of about three feet. At that range it looked bigger than the barrel of a shotgun. It looked a lot more like a cannon.

Chapter VII

The man back of the Hawken was old enough to be Buck Duane's grandfather or maybe even his grandfather's grandfather. "Older than sin and tougher than time," Captain MacNelly would have said. For all of that the hand that held the rifle was as steady as a rock, and the eyes that looked Duane over were keen and alive.

"Just set steady fer a minute," the patriarch said. "I been expectin' ye fer a long spell now."

"Put the gun down," Duane said, recovering himself. "There's no reason a couple of reasonable men can't talk things over."

"Hah," the oldster said. His long white beard jumped when he said it. He wore a dirty leather shirt that had once been fringed, woolen pants and high moccasins bound round the legs instead of boots. A flop-brimmed black felt hat, long since devitalized by usage and held together by thick grease, covered his head.

"Had. What makes you think me a reasonable man, bub? How do ye know I ain't just aimin' to shoot you off the back of that there horse animal and take you stuff fer my own? Answer me that."

It was a long time since anyone had called Buck Duane 'bub.' It amused him and he began to relax.

"I know it easy enough," he said. "Anybody that could make me walk right under his gun without my knowing he was alive could have shot me out of the saddle with no trouble at all. That's what he would have done too instead of risking my pulling one of my Colts before you could shoot."

The muzzle of the rifle lowered. "Durned ef I don't think ye'd have tried it too, if'n I really meant ye harm. Well, light and set. I been expectin' ye too long a while to waste good time with useless jawclabber now."

"Kept ye in sight ever since ye run round those two tarnation fools at the pass. Could have nailed ye any time, but that there ain't my meaning. I been expectin' you with my mind fer five years now. Sooner or later somebody had to come pokin' round about what goes on down there. Just had to. Now light and set easy. I got things to say."

Buck Duane swung down off Bullet's neck.

"Just why do you think I'm poking around?" he asked. "Mightn't I be just another saddlebum going through?"

The old man gave a snort that might have been either laughter or contempt, or perhaps a little of each and some other emotion for good measure. Duane couldn't tell.

"You ain't no saddlebum," he said, "nor neither are ye one of the wild bunch, though there's much the same stamp on you that outlaws have. Give me odds and I'll bet right here that ye're one a' them Texas Rangers. Am I right?"

"You're right," Duane said, "but how you did it is way out beyond me."

"Easy as he knew I wouldn't shoot," the other said, and spat tobacco juice in the dust, automatically burying it in the dirt with a flick of one foot to keep a tracker from seeing it. "I knew someday or other the folks outside would begin to wonder 'bout this valley. Mebbe one a them poor fools down thar writ a letter out. Anyway, when they wondered, they'd send somebody to see and report.

"Now who would they be most likely to

send in? The Governor? A Yankee school-marm? General William Tecumsah Sherman? Shecks no. Thar's only just one likely feller to drap by, and that would be a Texas Ranger. Right?"

"Right," Duane told him. "Are we safe to just sit here and jaw?"

"Safe as if we was perched up on the moon," the old man said. "I'm Lefty Wilder, mountain man." He said the last with pride. "I'm wilder than most by nature and by name. I trapped with Deef Smith when I were a mere lunker, and been in the mountains all my life."

"Glad to know you, Lefty," Duane said. "I'm Buck Duane, and like you figured, I'm a Ranger. You're the only person in High Valley that knows it except me."

"I ain't in High Valley nor want to be," the old man said. "So it's still your secret. I live up in the hills here. More comfortable that way, though the's might small hills to the Rockies where I trapped. Don't feel to comfortable with too many folks close by."

"I see that. Do you still trap?"

"Just when I want a skin fer myself. No market. 'Stead o' that I pan a leetle gold late years. Ain't much of the stuff in here, but enough to keep an old man like me in coffee and salt. Now you found the rustler's road, you going out again?"

"Not quite yet, old-timer," Duane said. "Two more things I need to know first, and I'd take kindly to any help you could give.

"Firstly, what is really back of the thing all the valley folk are so scared of? I mean what is this talk about killing the river?

"And last, but for sure not least, just who is this Mister Smith I hear talk of?"

Left Wilder scuffed the ground with the toe of his moccasin and chewed reflectively on a twig. "Fust question I know the answer to," he said then. "Camp with me tonight, and in the morning I'll take and show ye. As fer the second, that I don't rightly know any better'n them chicken-hearted ranchers do. You have to find that out fer yerself."

"I'd hoped you'd know," Duane said. "You must have seen the rustler's herds driven in and then ride out." He knew the old fellow's curiosity would have made that a cinch. "Who leads them?"

"Sometimes Neal Rogers rides," Lefty Wilder said, "he's the one ramrods the Rainbow for Ace. That is supposing that Ace Holden owns the Rainbow, which I don't think is so myself. A big, tough man –

prob'ly overdue fer hanging in three-four places."

"He is that," Buck Duane agreed. "The Rangers have a wanted notice on that name."

"Well, he's the one. Fast with a gun and damn-your-eyes in general. Ace never rides. Once er twice there was a feller with them might just be the one you want. Tall but not heavy, slim almost like a woman in man's clothes. City bought clothes. Always wore a neckerchief tied around his face. I thought it were to keep dust out of his nose, but it could just as well be a disguise."

"Ever see him anywhere else?" Duane asked. "Would you recognize him if you did?"

"No to both questions," Lefty Wilder said. "I ain't never heard his voice nor seen him off a horse. Might know him if he rode by with his mask on, but nary other way. Let's go now, bub. Camp's still a ways farther on."

Buck Duane left it at that. He mounted Bullet. Lefty Wilder whistled and a small shaggy mustang pony came out of the trees where he'd been feeding. He had a blanket cinched around his middle for a saddle and no stirrups. A rangy, long-haired mongrel dog as big as a wolf came with him and bared his fangs in a ritual snarl at Duane.

"Won't bite lessen I tells him," Lefty Wilder said. "Come on."

Duane fed the old man his storebought rations that night and in the morning. Wilder drank a whole pot of strong, boiled coffee sweetened with condensed milk.

After that they left the camp and rode north and east for some miles. With difficulty Duane restrained himself from asking the old fellow where they were going. He was content to know that the mystery of killing the river was shortly to be solved.

At mid-morning they rested their horses on a ridge of land. The river lay before them, coming down from the north and making a slow bend eastward towards the valley.

"This is where a river might be killed," Lefty Wilder said and pointed. "Not rightly killed as a river, but just as good as fer the valley folks. Look for yourself."

At this point Duane could look down on the ground below well enough so that he presently noticed what the old trapper wanted him to see.

The river was neither as wide nor as placid here as farther down its course, but still carried a good spate of water. It came out of a rather steep-walled canyon that ran almost due north-south.

Directly opposite the canyon mouth opened a rather broad valley split down the middle by the shelf of rock on which their horses rested. This height ran almost, but not quite to the mouth of the canyon. Canyon and the two branches of the valley thus formed a Y shaped figure, with the canyon for a trail. The river ran down the eastern arm of the Y.

Buck Duane saw however that the western pointing fell away more rapidly into the hills. At some time in the distant past an earthquake or other cataclysm of nature had broken the cliff where the river came out and tumbled masses of rock to block the root of the western arm. It was this barrier of fallen rock, rather than the natural lie of the land which determined that the river ran east instead of west from this point.

"Ye see it now, bub?" old Left Wilder asked.

"I see it," Duane said. "I ain't sure I believe it, but I see it. Somebody with money and a little engineering study could plant dynamite to blow through that ridge of loose rock and dirt."

"Pre-cisely," Wilder said. "Only need a

small channel to get her started. The water 'ud cut the rest. Fust thing anybody knows in the valley there's trout flapping in the sun where their nice sweet water used ta be. Coupla small feeder streams might still keep a trickle going, but there wouldn't be nothing left you could rightly call a river. Nothing at all."

Buck Duane sat his horse and thought.

"Once done," he mused aloud, "it would take an army and a dam to put the water back in its present channel. As far as High Valley's concerned that river would sure enough be dead, and so would the town and the ranches around it. No wonder Ace has them scared if he even hints at being able to turn the water to the west."

"Rain as rain," Lefty Wilder said. "Now that ye knows, bub, what'd you figure to do about all this?"

Duane didn't lose his aplomb.

"What I won't do," he said, "is monkey around down there or even go any closer. They may have sent somebody to watch it since they knew I was in the hills. Nothing could be done there anyhow."

"Right you are."

"So," Duane continued, "there's only one other thing I can do that could do any good at all. I've got to find this Mr. Smith. He's the top man, the hinge pin of this whole set-up. He's the one who'd give the order to blow that rock. Once I've got him under arrest, he'll have nor reason to do that. His cover'll be blown and his game spoiled anyhow."

"So you just go and arrest him," Lefty Wilder said. "I heerd ye Rangers was a mite tetched, and now I believe it. Before ye go making arrests, wouldn't it be a smart idee to find yer man? How ye going to do that, bub?"

Chapter VIII

Buck Duane left sugar, flour, coffee and salt with old Lefty Wilder to eke out his mountain food, and headed back towards the valley. He actually had only a very general idea of what he meant to do when he got there. To say he'd arrest Mister Smith was one thing, but to do it was a horse of another color. First he had to find the man.

By now Duane was pretty sure that Smith wasn't off someplace in the East. The whole operation was too big and too complicated for an absentee-landlord set up. That was particularly true with men like Ace Holden for subordinates. Nobody as smart as Smith seemed to be would trust Ace Holden to make major decisions in a time of emergency. He'd have to be on hand himself for fast consultation if trouble came up. that meant Smith had to be somebody in the valley itself. There was no other settlement less than a couple of days' ride away.

It might be a smarter Ace Holden, using

the blustering Ace roles as a cover to hide his real abilities. Or if so, why not Judge Gowanus? Nobody would suspect him of brains enough to uncork one of his own bottles. Doctor Dan Mills had the education and presence to organize this rustler's paradise and to see the shock value implicit in a threat to cut off the water. On the other hand why would a man like that get involved with crime in the first place? Why risk position and fortune and professional status against exposure and arrest?

It could be one of the townsmen or ranchers leading a double life. Even Sally Burke herself had the brains and courage needed. "Slender like a woman," old Lefty Wilder had said. Duane hated to think that might be the case, but he had to consider it.

There was another possibility he wanted to check out first. Quite simply it was that the mystery man might be a mystery only because he stayed permanently out at the Rainbow spread ranch complex. If he never went further into the valley itself and arrived and left by the rear door, the rustler's road, of course none of the other ranchers would know him by sight.

The Rainbow fence had always been a boundary line. Riders from the big ranch might and did come into town on Saturday nights for the dubious diversions offered by Ace's place, but it was all one-way traffic. Nobody from outside was welcome to pass the fence going in. As a matter of fact nobody wanted to.

Duane wanted a look at the residents of the big, two-story, timber and stone ranch house he'd so far seen only through his field glass.

Wanting and getting that look could be two very different propositions. As a rustler's hide-out the place would be closely guarded. There'd be more men staying there than were needed to look after the cattle and they'd be alert for trouble. Most of them would be gun hands and better at a fight than at regular ranch work.

People would be coming and going around the headquarters complex all day and far into the night. Chances were the only time he could get close enough to see an individual would be so late at night that everybody, including Smith, would be in bed. He couldn't identify a leader that way.

Well, there was no use in worrying about it in advance. Rangers were used to having to meet all sorts of sudden and extreme emergencies. On a wild and expanding frontier no officer of the law could operate by the book. Every situation had to be played by ear with the sole criterion that nothing was really impossible for a brave and determined man.

As it turned out Duane didn't have to solve that particular problem right away.

He took his time going back across the rustler's trail and scouting the country for the benefit of Captain MacNelly and his men. Lefty Wilder had told him the only good route into the Rainbow territory, except for the guarded rustler's pass, was on the west about three miles north of the ranch house. Here a good stand of trees offered cover from watchers and the shallow floor of an ancient, eroded down canyon, now just a long depression in the prairie, extended that cover until close to his objective. The old man had given him explicit directions as to the route he should follow, and he planned to arrive just before dark.

Duane spotted the improvised camp in a cluster of cottonwoods on the bank of a mere trickle of feeder stream, about five in the afternoon.

He could see that it had been carefully placed so that anyone coming in to the point he was heading for would have to see it. That made him wonder. A picket posted like the men at the notch to shoot him down would have gone to great pains to conceal a camp instead of putting it where he couldn't have missed it in case he came this way.

He took out his glass and carefully focused on the fire and the figure sitting by it. Then he saw that it was Ann Mills, the doctor's sister. That puzzled him even more. What was she doing out in the hills?

The idea came to him that she could have been put there solely as bait to lure him into a trap. He spent the next hour and a half making a wide circle around the campfire. He found her tracks, but only her tracks, leading into the little hollow where she was sitting. Duane was a competent tracker. If there was an ambush, then it was a one-woman affair.

He decided to ride on in to the fire. If she was waiting for him, he'd find out. If not, he could always keep her under observation till he decided what his next move ought to be.

She didn't even look up when she heard his horses coming in behind her. That meant either that she expected him or was dead sure anybody who might show up there would be a friend. He stopped Bullet only twenty feet or so from her back.

"It's Mr. Duane, isn't it?" she called out and then started to rise and turn in the same motion. "Light and set a spell, as you people out here say."

Natural caution made Duane scan the horizon once more even though he was sure there were no watchers. Then he dismounted.

"I saw your fire and recognized you," he said. "I thought I'd stop by and see if you needed anything."

"Of course you made doubly sure I was alone first," she said, and laughed as he tried to keep a poker face. "No, I didn't see you, if that makes any difference. I'm just sure a careful man like you would circle any camp before riding in – that is he would if he thought himself in hostile country."

Duane walked over and stood looking down at her. "And whyever would I think that, Miss Mills? Does Ace Holden's hand reach out this far?"

"Let's make it Ann and Buck," she said and sat down again. He sat beside her. "Leave the formality for my brother's drawing room, which is a stuffy place at best. To answer your question, Buck – yes, it reaches here and a lot further. I think you know that already, or you wouldn't be heading back towards the pass down to the Rainbow. Would you, now?"

Duane preferred to let her do all the answering.

"That's quite an assumption, Ann." He tried the name and found it good in his mouth. "What do you mean by it?"

"Oh," she said, "why can't we just be honest with each other? This one time at least – this one night? You really mean how much do I know about the doings at the Rainbow? I know a lot, kind sir. Maybe things that could help you."

She paused then and lit a thin, dark cigar, hardly larger than a cigarette, which she took from a silver-mounted leather case.

"Back East," she said, smiling, "women, even nice women, Buck, are allowed many privileges they aren't out here. Smoking alone or in the company of family or a close friend is sometimes one of them."

"Thank you," Duane said.

"Further thinking of you as a friend? I have a feeling I don't quite understand that somehow I'm the one who should feel honored by it. I wish that I had met you sooner, Buck."

Duane thought of the long, lonely outlaw years.

"You wouldn't have liked me," was all he said.

"Don't be too sure at all. I might even have loved you as an outlaw, though I'm perfectly sure I'd have hated a life on the dodge. I'm not made for that sort of life."

"What makes you think I was ever an outlaw?"

"Oh, my dear," she said. Haven't you realized yet that I know who Buck Duane is? I don't think my brother Dan realizes it yet, but I've heard of you. Half the West has. You were an outlaw because you killed a man, and now you're where you really belong. You're a Texas Ranger and defending the very law that tried so hard to bring you in to hang. It's no great secret."

"I wish it were," Duane said. "Who else in the valley knows?"

"I haven't gone around discussing it," she said. "I wanted to keep you all to myself. Seriously though, I don't really think anyone else knows. If Dan had recognized you, I think he would have mentioned it to me. The rest of our fellow citizens aren't overly bright. Or hadn't you noticed? If one of them knew, it would be all over town. Then you'd be in hostile territory for sure.

"So I think you and I are the only ones

who really know. So far it's our secret, and I'm as ready as you to let it stay that way."

"You'll have to tell me why," Duane said. "I'd like to know where everybody stands."

"You mean why do I Let you see how much I know?" she asked. "Of course you do. If I know so much about the Rainbow, doesn't that mean I'm one of them?"

"You can't really blame me," Duane said.

"Of course I don't blame you," she said. "You have to ask, and in good time I mean to answer. Not before we eat though. And don't tell me you're not hungry. I brought special things for us, and I'll taste them first so you'll know I haven't put poison in anything, not even the wine."

She actually had three bottles of good wine cooling in the little feeder stream. There was cold roasted chicken and smoked wild turkey and a ham and loaves of crusty home-made bread and cans and jars of other things Buck Duane hadn't tasted before.

As dusk fell, the fire shed a warm circle of light about the spot where they sat and the evening breeze of the high prairies murmured in the grass and riffled the high branches of the cottonwood trees. There was a moment of repletion and warmth and contentment for them both.

Then Ann Mills turned to him, her face serious in the flickering light of the sinking fire.

"Time to talk, Buck Duane," she said. "It's time for me to answer questions now. It's funny, I almost told you all this the other night after Dan tied up your arm, but then I thought you were going away out of all our lives anyway and there wouldn't be much point in it.

"Things would have been much simpler really if you had ridden on back to San Antonio or wherever it was they sent you from. Because you're still here some really nasty people are going to think they have to kill you. There's a lot of them, and they're tough. Good as you are with those big guns, I'm afraid they have a real chance of succeeding.

"How do I know all this? It's not any real mystery, and it doesn't mean I'm one of the gang. I'm not, you know. We found out, Dan and I, because he's a doctor. Soon after we came here he was called out to the Rainbow on more than one occasion. Always it was to treat men bad hurt with gunshot wounds.

"Dan is an intelligent man, and they couldn't blindfold him while he worked, could they? He saw enough to make a pretty good guess at what I'm sure you've already found out, that the Rainbow Ranch is really just a cover up for some big rustling operation. They in turn – oh, I suppose I might as well come right and say Ace Holden since I've said so much already – were also no fools. Ace knew Dan had been putting two and two together. They might have killed him then, as they killed others before and since, but they didn't.

"Dan is the only doctor within at least two hundred miles, and a rustler gang can certainly use a doctor to advantage. So instead of killing my brother they just set out to make sure that he would never give them away."

"How could they do that?" the Ranger asked. "A man like your brother – ."

"I know," she said. "Dan is all you imply. Wealthy, cultivated, college trained, an Easterner and a respected professional man, and a wonderful person besides.

"The trouble is, Buck, everybody has an Achilles' heel. That means an area where he's vulnerable, where he can be reached. Dan's no exception. He is, and always has been an insane, inveterate gambler. Why do you think we took what we could of what used to be the family fortune and came and buried ourselves in a wilderness like this? It was because Dan was running away from staggering gambling debts back home.

"Ace Holden used his connections to find out about those debts. He went East and bought Dan's I.O.U.'s for a few cents on the dollar. They're locked in his safe now."

"That's one way to hold a gambler," Duane admitted.

"It's not the only one. They let him gamble any time he wants in Ace's place – on credit. In the time since we got here, he's lost almost thirty thousand dollars more than he wins. So you see why he does their medical work and keeps his mouth shut. He hates it. We both do, but he can't help himself."

Duane had his own opinion in regards to her last statement, but he decided to keep it to himself. Instead he asked another question.

"Suppose you tell me the one thing more I need to know," he said. "Just who is Mister Smith?"

She looked him right in the face and her own eyes in the firelight were wide and guileless. Her voice had the ring of sincerity. "Buck, I honestly don't know. I'm terribly sorry. I'd tell you if I could. I'll say who I think it is, but that's all I can give you is my own opinion."

"All right," Duane said, hiding his disappointment, "then suppose you make your guess and tell me why you make it. That could be a help."

"I can't prove it," she said, "but I'm logically and morally sure Mister Smith is Ace Holden. Oh, I know Ace talks about getting instructions and waiting for orders, but it's just talk. Nobody's ever seen this mystery boss of his. At least no one ever admitted to it that I know. I think 'Smith' is just somebody Ace made up so the valley people wouldn't hold him personally responsible for everything his men do. Like what the Old Testament would call a scapegoat – only in this case it isn't even a real scapegoat but just a shadow. Just something Ace made up to hide himself behind."

She didn't know it, but her words were convincing Buck Duane that some of his own thinking had been correct.

"All right, I think you may be right," he said. "Only on thing – you know Ace a lot better than I do. Has he got the brains to plan something like this and carry it through?"

"I think so," she said. "Ace is self-educated, but crime is his speciality. He knows it inside out. He may not be an intelligent man in the same way that Dan is, but he's tricky and shrewd and used to living by his wits. Now is that all you have to ask me tonight?"

"No," Duane said. "There's the question you know I've got to ask. Why do you tell me all this, with your own brother involved at least as an accessory? Ace Holden can ruin you both, strip you of everything you own if he finds out. You still tell me all this. Why?"

"That was the question I waited for," Ann said. "I thought up answers that would make me look noble and honest and brave, but now that you're here, face to face like this, I can't lie to you. I'll tell it just the way it really is. I've got a reason for telling you, a selfish reason, and I'm going to ask a price.

"You've probably guessed the reason. The only way I can see for Dan to get out from under this blackmail is to have the Rangers break up the gang and arrest or kill Ace Holden."

"I can guess the price, too," Duane said. "You want your testimony to buy your

106

brother out." She nodded. "Maybe it can at that. It will certainly help, but I'm not the one who can promise you how much. I'm only a Ranger. What happens to your brother will be up to a judge. Had you thought about that?"

She put out her hand and took hold of his wrist. Even at that moment her touch was both strong and caressing. "Yes, I'd thought of that. So I want more than your promise to help. I want you to go with me tomorrow and get those I.O.U.'s out of Ace's safe. I know the combination. I stole a copy of it the night you had the gunfight, while Ace was talking to you and was careless. Didn't you wonder how I came to be in the hotel that night?

"I can get you into the safe, Buck. Anything else you find there, and there should be plenty, you can keep for evidence. Just let me take the markers, and forget about Dan when the arrests come. Will you do it, Buck? Will you, darling?"

The moon had risen and the fire was dying. The night was alive with the smell and rustle of living, growing things. There under the big trees by the little stream, it was cool and pleasant.

Duane sat quietly for a time before

answering. Then he said: "Supposing the facts are what you say, and you can help me get enough evidence to expose and arrest the real Mr. Smith, then I reckon your brother's medical services don't have to be brought to anybody's attention."

She leaned over and kissed him. It wasn't a warm and grateful kiss, but the hot and passionate lips of a woman fully aroused that he felt. Involuntarily, his arms tightened about her. Later – much later – they rolled up in their separate blankets and slept.

Chapter IX

In the morning Buck Duane and Ann Mills talked over their plans for getting hold of the papers.

Duane had another question then. "If Ace really is the rustler king, why would he keep anything incriminating in town? Wouldn't he figure it'd be safer out at the Rainbow?"

Ann just laughed at him.

"Exactly the opposite," she said. "The last people in the world Ace Holden is going to trust with really important information or evidence about anything at all are his own men. He's probably cheating them on their share of the take anyway. And even if that's not so, look at the hold it would give them for blackmail.

"No, Buck, he'll have everything important right in the hotel safe where he spends most of his own time and where he can keep his eye on it personally."

Duane accepted that statement without argument. He was relieved that he didn't have to try sneaking into the heavily guarded ranch house.

They swung wide of the Rainbow land and came back into the valley a couple of miles the other side of the fence.

"Don't you think I should ask for help from some of the ranchers?" Duane asked. "These aren't big spreads, maybe two or three riding hands apiece, but if they'd back us, the job would be a simple one." He wanted to see what she'd say.

"You know better than that, darling," Ann said.

She was smoking one of her small cigars and her long hair blew in the wind. The stetson she wore was cocked at a rakish angle and her breasts strained the fabric of her linen blouse. She wore the long skirt split into two much oversized trouser legs and boots.

"If you think seeing just one Ranger here will put heart in those spineless sheep after six years of fear, you're making an awful mistake. The only time they'll come out in the open is after you've got Ace behind bars."

It was the answer he'd expected her to give – indeed the same he'd have had to give himself, if their roles had been reversed. He

110

knew the valley ranchers had to protect their water at just about any cost.

If the rock slide was ever actually blown, or if Smith were to attempt a foreclosure of the whole valley at one time, they would probably rise in desperation. Now with the rationalizations of years still in their mouths and the widow Bass's tears still wet on her cheeks, the best he could hope for was an uneasy neutrality. Accordingly he and Ann stayed back from the river all day as they rode. As far as they could tell nobody saw them pass.

They planned to ride into town after dark but still early enough so the saloon might not be crowded. They'd go into the place by the back door, and put a gun in Ace's belly. If he refused to open the office door for them, Buck would break it down or shoot the lock off. Ann would use the safe combination to open it quickly.

With speed and luck they could be in and out, with Ace as a prisoner, before anyone else realized what the raid was all about.

"From there on, I'll take it," Duane said. "Once I get him in San Antone with evidence to convict, your troubles will be over."

They rode up to town in the full dark that

follows a summer twilight before the moon gets over the horizon. They left their horses in a clump of brush near an old tumbledown shack and walked the last hundred yards to the rear of Ace's saloon.

"That's his office window," Ann pointed. "It's dark now, so he must still be out front at the bar."

The window had heavy iron bars bolted to its frame. Otherwise Duane would have gained entrance to the office by that route.

Nobody saw them go into the back door. They tried the office door and found it locked.

"No help for it now," Duane said in a low tone. "We'll have to get him out of the bar."

"He knows me," she said. "I can get him to come back here easier than you can."

"Is he used to entertaining you in the office?" Duane asked. She shook her head indignantly. "Then I'm the one to fetch him back. I've got a couple of powerful arguments to convince Mister Ace he better come." He tapped his gun butts.

"All right," she said. "Don't fail. Oh, Buck, darling, don't fail me now." She spoke in a low tone and a burst of piano music from the big room almost drowned out her words.

Buck Duane walked the few steps up the narrow hall. A strange chill of premonition touched his spine and that old knot of twisted cold was in his stomach. The killing chill he called it and it always came when a gunfight was near.

He opened the door and went in. The room was full of light and the piano was tinkling and banging away, but there were only a few customers at the bar. At this early hour only one of the hotel girls had come downstairs. She was the first to see and recognize Duane.

She opened her mouth to scream.

Ace Holden was at the bar with his back to the door, talking to a customer. One of the two gunsels Buck had seen before was on his boss' other side tilting a glass of whiskey to his mouth.

The other gun Duane had seen was at the same table they'd used before, dealing himself a hand of solitaire.

The woman's scream froze everyone in the room and stopped the piano. It was as if a movie had suddenly stopped on a single frame, except that these were real people in a real place.

The gunman standing beside Ace Holden was the first person in the big room to recover. He opened his hand dropping the whiskey glass to smash on the floor, and dug for his gun. The need to stop and then reverse the direction of his hand slowed him down.

Duane out-drew the man easily and shot him through the upper right arm. The big bullet splintered the bone so he'd never use a gun with that hand again.

His partner got halfway up from the table. When he saw Duane's smoking gun swing his way, he put his hands up.

"Hold it!" Duane said. His voice carried clearly through every part of the room. "Next person makes a move Ace gets the top of his head shot off. I've no business with the rest of you. Stay quiet and you won't get hurt."

"He means it," Ace Holden yelled, his voice cracking on a high squeal of fright. "Nobody move, for God's sake." Then to Duane: "What do you want with me? I'm not armed. I wouldn't draw on you if I was."

"Ace Holden," Duane said icily. "In the name of the Law and of the State of Texas I place you under arrest on a charge of cattle rustling and murder. Come along peaceably or I take you anyway."

"Arrest me! Me? You're crazy. What

authority have you to arrest anyone?"

"Full authority of the Law," Buck Duane said to the room at large. "I'm a Texas Ranger."

"Oh, my God." It was the woman's voice. "A Ranger."

"A Ranger?" someone in the back of the room said. "You know what that means, boys? Now God help us all."

Two men in the room stirred uneasily. One of them wearing the sweat-soiled shirt and high boots of a rancher called out then: "You, Ranger. Man, you don't know what you'll do to this whole valley if you take that man."

"Come on, Ace," Duane said. "Into your office."

There was a murmur from the men as Ace Holden still held back, and then confused voices. "We can't let him do it."

"Stop the Ranger."

"Rescue Ace."

"Move," Duane said to Holden, "or I'll kill you where you stand. Now." He gestured with his gun.

Ace Holden looked at the Ranger and knew then that he was seeing death itself. He started to move slowly towards the door. He said: "Don't shoot, boys. He means it." His

115

voice was almost a bleat like that of a sacred sheep. Whatever else Ace Holden may have been, he was surely no fighting man.

Buck Duane moved after him, trying to watch Holden and the whole room at the same time.

"You men don't interfere," he said at the door. "Obstruct an officer in the execution of his duty, and you'll have a full Ranger troop here in a week to hunt you down." That stopped them for the moment.

Ace Holden himself put up no fight at all. He went down the hall to the door of his office. When he saw Ann Mills standing there he went white as a sheet and his big mouth gulped air like a fish out of water. He looked as if he wanted to say something, but couldn't quite make it.

"Hello, Ace," she said. "It's my turn now, isn't it? Just keep your mouth shut and cooperate and hope you stay alive. Don't make any mistakes now. Get this door unlocked."

Ace Holden did as he was told and then gave Duane his ring of keys. Ann went to the safe, consulted a slip of paper from her pocket and spun the dial right and left. There was a confused murmur of voices from the hallway outside the closed door.

"What's going on?" they heard.

"He's got Ace in there. He's going to arrest him. Didn't you hear him say he was a Ranger?"

"Ranger? Then Smith will – Oh no."

Ann got the safe open. There were a couple of tin dispatch boxes inside. When she opened the first one it was full of money, mostly bills and ten and twenty dollar gold pieces. She just turned that out on the table to see if there were papers underneath. There weren't and she left the money where it had fallen.

The second box was locked, but one of Ace Holden's keys opened it. This one was full of legal papers, notebooks, envelopes, and the like. She started to dig into the pile.

"Better hurry up," Duane said. "I don't want that crowd to get any crazy ideas."

"They haven't got the guts, darling," Ann said. "Besides, it'll only take a minute to find what I want."

Buck Duane went to the door and cracked it open. The men in the hallway fell over each others' feet backing out of the hall into the bar again.

"You're making a mistake, Ranger," Ace Holden said behind Duane's back. "I'm not the one you want."

There was a sudden crashing shot that sounded like a cannon in the small office. Buck whirled to see Ace Holden standing with a dazed and uncomprehending look on his face while blood poured out to stain his shirt front over the heart. Ann had fired her big forty-four caliber derringer into him at a range of about two feet. He was dead before he hit the floor.

Ann Mills looked from the body to Duane.

"He went for his gun," Ann said. "When your back was turned. He grabbed for a hidden gun. At least I couldn't take a chance it was anything else. He'd have shot you in the back."

"I needed that man for a witness," Duane said. "Why couldn't you have just winged him?"

He knelt over Holden's body and searched. There was a pearl-handled thirty-two rimfire in a belt holster right at the small of his back. He could have decided to try for it, but Duane began to wonder. It wasn't like Ace Holden.

"We've got to hurry," Ann reminded him. She shoved the tin box of papers into his hand. "There's your evidence. Enough to hang the whole Rainbow crew. Believe me it's all there."

There were loud voices in the hall. Duane opened the door wide enough to let Ann follow him through, but not enough so the men outside could see Ace Holden on the floor. He had the box in his left hand and his gun in his right.

With a show of calm Duane holstered his gun and shut and locked the door with his right hand. He was betting the men weren't worked to anything like a killing rage as yet. He was right. They hesitated and then started back towards the bar once more.

Ann and Duane walked down the hall in the opposite direction towards the rear door of the building.

There was sudden thunder of fast running ponies in the main street of town, and a wild burst of yelling. It sounded to the Ranger as if at least a couple of dozen riders were coming hell bent for leather.

Ann tugged at his arm.

"He's done it," she yelled. "Oh, damn him, damn him, damn him. He's done it. Run."

"Done what?"

"Sent in the Rainbow riders. Run, darling. Run for the horses."

She dropped his arm and ran like a deer for the shed where their horses were tied.

She didn't make it. Most of the riders pulled up their horses in the street fronting the hotel and bar, but one, either bolder or smarter than the rest came right around into the yard behind. He rode with reins in his teeth, guiding his pony with knee and spur and waving a big forty-five in each hand.

Ann's running figure caught his eye, and he started firing both guns as he came. She screamed and lurched and went down in the mud.

Buck Duane shot the man out of his saddle. The horse went on to circle the hotel and rejoin its mates in front.

Duane felt as if he was running slow-motion like something in a nightmare, but it was probable that he'd never in his life moved as fast as he did right then. When he got to Ann there was blood all over her linen blouse. All he could see was blood and mud and her face rigid with shock, the eyes wide open and blank.

He swung her up over his shoulder. She still held on to the two thick envelopes she'd taken from the tin box. He ran as fast as the high-heeled boots would let him for the shelter of the shed. Once inside he set her down with infinite gentleness against the wall. He unfastened the buttons of the bloody shirt.

She's been shot through the left side of the stomach. The bullet had gone on out of the back without hitting bone, but God only knew what else had been torn up by its passage.

For the moment shock, mercifully was sparing her pain.

He took his neckerchief and hers and made a rude bandage; after first putting a pad made of strips torn from her shirt over each wound. It might stop the bleeding. For the moment it was all he could do.

The noise at the hotel had quieted down, and Duane knew this meant there'd be a rush in short order. The shed had been built a long time before as a crude stable. The rear and side walls were of heavy tree-nailed plank. There were wide doors in front which he left open; and in front of the place the fairly stout remains of a rail and pole fence. There was a growth of weed and new brush on the right and rear of the shack where the ground sloped down to the river. In front there was almost a clear reach of level ground to the hotel, one hundred yards away.

Duane had his own carbine and a near twin from Ann's saddle sheath. He checked that both were loaded and sat down to wait. There was a heavy wooden horse trough in the small corral space outside the shack and he used this as cover, figuring the rustlers would follow a natural inclination to shoot into the cabin through the open doors and overlook where he lay. The night left the cabin and its yard in shadow while the lights of the hotel and street would silhouette any attacker for his sights.

Within five minutes guns were firing at the shack from the windows in both floors of the hotel. Duane stayed quiet and made no reply. If they wanted to waste lead on the heavy timbers, he didn't care to stop them.

Shortly after that he saw the back door of the hotel out of which he and Ann had run begin to ease open. When it was fully open he fired into the doorway. A wild yell and the sudden slam of the door told him he'd made a hit.

At that the snipers in the windows opened up as fast as they could pump the levers of their Winchesters. A regular hail of lead harmlessly pelted the old shack. Duane held his fire.

Duane's first two shots knocked down the

men coming from his left. One of them got up and came on again. It took Duane two more shots to bring him down again.

By this time the two from the right were closing distance fast. If they hadn't made the twin mistakes of stopping to fire at him and trying to run in high-heeled boots, they'd have been right on top of him.

Duane shot the lead man at such close range the powder blast almost scorched his shirt.

That was too much for number four. He swung wide of the corral and ducked around the corner of the shack. Duane came after him at a crouching run, but the man was already hidden in the brush and crashing his way downslope to the river.

The Ranger pointed rather than aimed in the direction of the sound and fired. He heard the sodden 'thunk' of the bullet hitting flesh and then a brief thrashing about, suddenly stilled.

For the moment, that was all. Even the men in the hotel stopped firing for lack of a real target to aim at. Just then the moon rose and shed silvery light across High Valley. With that light to aid Duane's already deadly shooting another rush on the shack would have been suicidal and everyone knew it.

Buck Duane slipped back into the shack. It was darker here, but he could see Ann still sitting where he'd left her, with her back propped against the wall. The shock was wearing off now, and pain was tearing at her all along the track of the wound. Her teeth bit into her lip, but she uttered no sound except for an occasional low moan.

"Good girl," Duane said. "Just hold on. We'll get out of this."

Ann shook her head and spoke with difficulty. "You will. Not me. I'm dying."

"No," Duane protested. "No. I'll parley with those men. They'll have to let your brother take you out of here and treat you. No man would refuse – ."

She held up one hand to stop him. "They might let him, but . . . couldn't . . . make him come . . ."

"Oh God," Duane said beginning to lose his control. "What are you talking about? Your own brother."

"You don't understand darling. Dan is my husband, not my brother."

Duane took that news almost as if it were a wound. He flinched. Ann looked as if she was about to faint. A little blood ran from

124

the corners of her mouth. He wiped it away with a cloth, and she looked at him and smiled.

"You see, darling. It's all over now. You can't fool me about dying. I'm too close. Dan won't save me if he could. Who do you think sent the riders in to kill us both? He did."

The horses, tethered inside the shack, shifted and stamped. It reminded Duane and he got his canteen off Bullet's saddle horn and offered her water.

She shook her head. "Not for stomach wound, darling. Must talk before I die. I'm sorry, Buck. It could have been wonderful for us, if only – ."

"It still will be," he burst out desperately. "I don't care what you – ."

"No," Ann interrupted. "Let me talk, dear. So little time. If I hadn't married Dan – He is your Mister Smith. Ace Holden just the front to mask us. Us. It was both our idea. After he fled in East.

"I told him I could meet you coming out and I give you papers involving Ace. Take . . . attention from us. Ace was beginning to blackmail us. Time to get rid of him."

Ann held up her hand and offered the

envelopes to him. "I'd hold out papers involving us. Nobody knew except a couple of rustlers and Ace Holden.

"It would have worked except there was more to it than that. Last night I knew I loved you. More than I ever felt for Dan. For just a little while I thought I could go away with you. Foolish. Had to pay for everything I've done, like this. Guess I knew all along.

"Dan must have guessed or maybe just suspicious. He sent the Rainbow riders in to kill us both."

Suddenly Ann's eyes widened and her right hand flashed up with the derringer. She fired so close to Duane's face that he felt the powder burn. The man who had sneaked up to the shack door while Buck Duane was distracted took the bullet in his heart and fell backwards out the door.

The shock and action was too much for Ann Mills.

"Everybody gets a chance at one decent thing," she said.

Then her body heaved and a rush of blood came out of her mouth. Duane reached out to catch her, but she slipped sideways, utterly limp. In seconds he was holding only a lifeless body.

For a long moment there was absolute

silence while Buck Duane looked at the pale, dead face of the woman who had loved him so briefly and so well.

Then the Ranger reloaded all his guns. He was going to get out of the shack and go up to the hotel and kill every man he found inside. For the first time, Buck Duane wanted to kill, to wipe out everyone who'd been a part of this terrible thing.

His own safety didn't matter any more, or his duty as a Ranger. "If I wait for them," he thought, "sooner or later they'll think to burn me out. They won't expect me to come up there. I'll go down through the brush and under cover of the river bank till I can cut up to the street. Half of them will die before they even know I'm there." It was the route he'd planned to use for escape from the valley before Ann was hit. Duane gathered himself for action.

It was then that the silence was shattered. There were riders pouring into town from the north and west. Rifle, pistol and shotgun fire broke out on the far side of the hotel from him. He could hear men yell and scream in pain, and then it was over.

A voice called out from the hotel: "You can come up, Ranger. The rustlers are dead or taken. Come up, and bring the woman with you."

Buck Duane brought her, lying limp and dead in his arms.

The new force were the valley ranchers and their hands. When the fighting started only one person in town had kept her head. That was Sally Burke. She'd saddled her horse and ridden for help. Most of the men were at a meeting in respect to the dead Bill Bass. The minister was holding services in the Bass ranch house only a few miles out of town.

When they heard the news, the men forgot their fears in a burst of desperate resolve and poured into town to rescue the Ranger and shoot it out with the rustlers regardless of the cost. They'd hardly dared to hope that Duane would still be alive.

"Where's Doctor Mills?" the Ranger asked, dry-eyed and hard.

"He rode out of town as we rode in," someone said. "He must have heard us coming. Kind of strange at that for a Doc to run from wounded men."

"He's your Mr. Smith," Duane said, "and he knows I've got the truth. I'll get him for you."

"He's gone to kill the river," said a voice that hushed the rest.

"He's riding to his death," Duane said. "Somebody fetch the horses up from the shack. I know where he's heading, and I'll bring him back. Don't worry about your river. He can't do the job alone. Just clean things up here, and wait for me."

Duane drove his horses without mercy all that night. At dawn he passed the Rainbow ranch without anyone trying to stop him. The men were dead or prisoners in town. The doctor had gone by a little before, a Mexican serving woman told him.

"He ride up big cow road."

That would be the rustler's trail.

Duane rode after him. He had three mounts, counting Ann's fine bay mare and he'd been shifting from one to the other all night. They were still fresh. He'd come up to Doctor Mills sometime that day, and when he did the doctor was a dead man. No trial for this one. No prison. No fast death by the spine-cracking hangman's rope. "I'll gut shoot him as she was shot," Duane had never felt like this before. The old, cold knot in his guts was a flaming hot coal now. He burned with the need for vengeance in a way that it would frighten him to remember later on.

The morning sun came up, brassy hot, before Duane came to the rustler's pass. By its rays Duane saw horses and a standing figure right at the mouth of the pass. He took out his field glasses for a look. Then the figure which had been so tense relaxed and slumped in the saddle.

When he rode up, old Lefty Wilder was sitting on a rock smoking his stub of a pipe and watching his mustang pony graze with the doctor's big black stallion.

Doctor Dan Mills – Mister Smith – lay just where the bullet that pulverized his heart had knocked him out of the saddle. He did not look graceful or important or deadly any more.

"I kind of thought ye'd be along, bub," Lefty Wilder said and spat towards the corpse. "Been watching this place since we said good-by before."

Duane got off his horse and sat down.

"I wanted that one for myself," he said through dry lips. "I needed that one."

"Better that I got him then," Lefty Wilder said. "Man gets no good from a personal shooting.

"I figgered ye and the young lady would

stir up a mess down there when I seen ye together. After that sombody'd be along to blow the river or to save his own neck, and he'd be the one you'd want most of all. So I figgered to wait here and sort of persuade him to linger till you came. This feller tried for his gun."

Buck Duane got his canteen and drank some water. The canvas case showed a stain of Ann Mills' blood where he had held it gently to her mouth.

"The young lady's dead, old-timer," Duane said in a voice hoarse with emotion.

"Lucky fer this rider he saw me first," Lefty Wilder said with understanding. He got off the rock and whistled to his mustang. When the pony trotted over, the old man got on his back.

"I know," he said in farewell. "Sometimes a man just needs to be alone."

Lefty Wilder left Buck Duane with the body of the man Captain MacNelly had sent him to find.

THE LONG TRAIL
TO NOWHERE

Chapter I

The Ranger captain's face was stern. "It's trouble, Buck," MacNelly said. "Bad trouble – like a wound that can bleed this whole State of Texas white, unless we manage to stop it in time."

Buck Duane had no doubt now of the importance of the mission he was being given.

The San Antonio office of the Texas Rangers was not an important-looking building. It was just another one-story adobe, not far from the historic Alamo on a street of saloons, gunsmiths' and saddlers' shops, wooden sidewalks and false fronts; all blanketed this day by searing Texas sun and all-pervading, wind-driven dust.

To a casual observer, MacNelly was as undistinguished-looking as the street itself. A wiry little man, all rawhide and spring steel, he wore no uniform or insignia of rank. His trousers were old and tucked into a pair of soft, high-heeled boots. He wore a leather jacket over a faded blue denim shirt and a knotted silk kerchief served both for tie and mask against trail dust and winter wind. The heavy revolvers belted around his waist were no different from those worn by a hundred casual passers-by in the street outside.

Only the eyes – keen, questing, intelligent, determined eyes – marked him as a leader among strong and passionate men. They were a sign of command far more meaningful than tailored cloth or epaulets could have been for a lesser man.

MacNelly sat behind a plain oak table upon which a map of West Texas had been spread out and pointed to it with one sun-browned hand.

"There it is," he said, and indicated a line that had been drawn in ink. "That's the new cattle drive found and marked by Charlie Goodnight and Ollie Loving back in sixty-six. You notice how it swings south and west of the Llano Estacado to avoid the worst of the Indian war parties of those days, and then goes north roughly along the lie of the Pecos River all the way to Colorado. Much of that route is in New Mexico Territory and no concern of ours, but the first few hundred miles from Port Concho are very much our business. That's where the trouble is."

"I see," Buck Duane said, leaning forward to follow the captain's finger.

Duane was a tall man and a quiet man, yet with the deadly quiet of Vesuvius in the instant before eruption. His eyes matched the captain's, his frame was spare and powerful, his hands long fingered and graceful. This was a man forever tensed and ready for instant action, yet with the soft-spoken ease of one fully assured of his own ability to handle any crisis.

He wore the heavy shirt and woolen pants, the high boots and pointed, wide-brimmed Stetson hat of the frontiersman. His two guns hung low and were tied down to the leg to make possible a fast and deadly draw in emergency.

"Maybe you do see," Captain MacNelly said. "Let me go over it anyways. Rustlers have been raiding the ranchers near the start of the trail. Herds waiting to go north have been hit just before the start. Others have left Fort Concho and never been heard of again. It's rustling combined with raiding on a big scale – a very big scale. Unless we can stop it, that whole trail north will be unusable. The ranchers out there will be left with no market for their steers."

"Can't you cut off the market for the stolen stock and break up the whole operation that way?" Duane asked.

"We could," the Captain said, "except that we don't know where the market is. The stolen steers and horses go roughly south and west into some of the wildest country and the face of the earth. That much we know. What we don't know is where they come out again or who sells them on the other end. That's going to be your assignment this time, to find out."

Duane looked at the map. "That won't be much help," he said quizically. It was a statement of fact. Except for few entries bracketed with question marks, that part of the map was a blank.

"You'll have to fill in most of those blanks for yourself and us," Captain MacNelly agreed. "Most of the area there was Commanche country – that and Comanchero. Up till the last few years no white man could keep his hair for a week in there unless he was Comanchero and renegade. The Indians and renegades brought their war parties east along the secret trails through the Staked Plains.

"They took their booty and captives back the same way to bases we haven't found to

138

this day. Forty years ago it was big business. Caravans of booty and slave buyers came up from Mexico to buy and go South again. The Comancheros were white renegades who rode with the redskins."

"Could they be at the bottom of this?"

"Not likely, Buck. That was a long time ago. The army broke up the trade back before the War. Most of the Comancheros were killed then. A few took their money to Mexico. Some may have stayed with the Indians. I don't envy them. Most are dead by now."

"Yes," Duane said, "but I'll have to go into their country anyhow."

"That's right. I hate to ask you, and the Lord knows what you'll find there. We've suspected the old Comanchero trails were being used by this rustler outfit. The trouble is, we can't find any trace of herds that size appearing in Mexico. It's not a matter of a few moseyhorns. Steers by the thousand and horses too are going somewhere. There'd have to be a trace if it was into Northern Mexico."

"It seems likely, Captain. Well, there's just one way to find out. I'll have to join up with the rustlers and go with them on a drive. If I live – and I think I will – I'll get back to you."

"I know you will," the Ranger officer said. "Just try not to take too many chances this time out. In spite of what some people think, we're law officers first and last and not glory boys. Go through with the drive if you have to. Once we know the route and the market, we can break up this operation. It doesn't need a one-man stand."

Buck Duane's lips curled in one of his rare, warm smiles. "Right you are, Captain. You may remember I took all the long chances any man could ask for when I was on the other side of the badge . . . back when I was an outlaw, before you gave me a second chance to be a human and a citizen."

"It's a chance you've more than made good, Buck," the captain said. "You know I'll never regret the moment you shook my hand and joined the Rangers."

"Neither will I," Duane said. "No one will ever know how much it's meant to me. I'll do my level best to do this job for you."

Chapter II

A week later Buck Duane rode west across the endless, empty West Texas plains. Man and horse – his favorite mount, big Bullet – were like a single living entity, the glorious beast seemingly guided by the rider's very thought more than by rein or spur. The setting sun sent golden bands across a velvet carpet of prairie grass tall enough to brush the rider's heels and the horse's belly.

Duane rode at peace with the world and himself. His immediate goal was a cottonwood-fringed stream bank a couple of miles ahead where he would camp for the night. The eyes of his mind went further ahead than that, to the time when he would have earned the right to a ranch of his own – perhaps even a wife to love and a son to teach to ride and shoot and to bear himself like a man.

Buck Duane was the son of a gunslinger who had been a living legend in his day. Men said Duane had pulled trigger twice after a rival's bullet had torn his heart. His son had inherited the legend, the deadly skill with a gun, and the wild pride that had made him kill an enemy in turn and seek the endless exile that the outlaw gunman knows. Only a stubborn refusal to debase himself by a murder, rape and robbery and the faith of a Ranger officer had saved him from a lonely death as climax to a wasted life.

His thoughts went back long years to his first campfires on the outlaw trail when the ghost of the man he'd killed came back to make a horror of the dark.

Suddenly his attention was forcibly pulled back to the present by the sight of a thin whisp of smoke rising above the very grove of cottonwoods towards which he was riding. It was only a trace a less keen-eyed man might not have seen at all. Whoever built the fire had made it small, and used dry wood that would give out a minimum of smoke.

All the more reason for caution. Now that the Indians were mostly driven to the west and the frontier pushed on a hundred miles with them, an honest rider or settler was not afraid to show sign in these parts. A furtive fire meant furtive men – and furtive men were dangerous men. No one needed to tell that to Buck Duane.

He pulled his repeating Winchester rifle from its leather saddle scabbard, and circled Bullet so as to approach the camping spot from downwind, where no tethered mount or Indian dog would scent him and give warning.

Because of the cottonwoods and because the ground dipped down to the streambed, Duane couldn't see the campsite unless he rode right up to it. by the same token the people there could not see him, either, unless they'd thought to post a guard.

Apparently they hadn't, and this set Duane's mind more at ease. Outlaws or raiding Indians would have spotted him at once, but his trained eye and ear detected no sign of an alert. He finally decided the chances of an ambush were too slight to stop him from riding in, and pulled Bullet out of the tall grass onto what appeared to be a trail running close to the smoke. He deliberately let the bit and spurs jingle and his mount's shoes pound on harder ground.

As he had intended, the men around the fire heard him coming in time to look him over. When they showed themselves on higher ground, he realized they would not make a first hostile move. He grinned to himself. He wanted to contact men of the owlhoot trail who could guide him to the rustlers he sought.

The men who stood at the edge of the cottonwood grove seemed to fill the bill. There were only two of them and they were watching him warily as he rode up the trail. Their backs were to the westering sun, which gave them some advantage, but Duane was not afraid.

The elder and heavier of the pair was a typical frontier hardcase with a month's-long curl of black beard and a broken nose. His clothing was black and shiny from the undisturbed accumulation of grease, smoke and dirt. He wore a single holstered Colt and carried a double barreled, cap-fired shotgun sawed off for ease in handling. At short range this could be a deadly weapon against beast or man.

His companion was slender and much younger, in fact hardly more than a boy. He wore a broad brimmed, low crowned 'farmer's' hat, a blue and white checked shirt, worn denim Levi's grown tight against his swelling thighs and an old pair of boots which must once have belonged to a bigger man. "He can take two steps before the boots move," Duane thought and grinned to himself.

The boy's gun was another matter. It was a beautiful weapon, carefully oiled, tied down with a rawhide thong, and with the plain wooden butt worn smooth from handling and notched like Duane's own. "He inherited that," the Ranger decided, "from a gunslinging pa. Just like I did my own."

He was close enough now that he pulled up his horse and held out both hands with palms open to show that he came in peace.

"Stop right thar, stranger, and git down," the older man called. "Who are you and where do you ride?"

The implied threat brought that old familiar fighting chill to Duane's body and mind. His muscles tensed as adrenalin poured into his blood. His arms and hands swung easily, ready to draw and fire. He knew he could kill both men without trouble, but some wild, hidden thing within him craved to put it to the test.

For the ten thousandth time he cursed that killer instinct in his brain and breast and brought it under iron control. He forced his teeth to part and his lips to smile.

"Let's all relax, boys," he called out. "I

wear no badge and I carry no quarrel. The way you show smoke there, if I meant harm I could've crept round and bushwhacked the pair of you an hour ago."

The boys looked startled. The older man didn't. "Maybe you could," he said. "Maybe not. No man's done it yet, for sure." He let the muzzle of the shotgun drop to point at the ground.

"I come in peace," Duane said, and made an Indian sign well known among the badlands outlaws.

The fellow recognized it and relaxed. "Why didn't you say so?" he asked. "Ride in to the fire, then. We've meat and coffee but no sugar nor flour. Welcome to share."

"I've plenty of both," Duane said, "I left San Antone in a hurry but stocked up at a crossroads store on the way. Welcome to share."

He gave Bullet a meager ration of oats and then hobbled him to graze the tall, nutritious grasses. He left the saddle on his mount's back, but loosed the cinch a bit. He carried his rifle and saddlebags to the fire, got out flour and sourdough and made biscuits for them all.

All three fell to with good appetite, but the boy ate like a ravening wolf. Buck Duane figured he had been on the run long enough to find the days long and the rations short. His partner tried to slow him down.

"A meal's a meal and enough's enough," he said, half to the kid and half in apology to Duane. "No restaurant on tomorrow's trail."

"I didn't think." The boy pushed back his plate in embarrassment. "I'll take less next time."

Buck Duane laughed. "I've enough for a day or so," he said. "Might as well eat. We're none of us headed for California this trip, I think."

"Oh, no," the boy said suddenly. "We'll find friends sooner than that."

His partner almost hit him. Duane moved to stop it. "I'm looking for friends myself," he said. "Friends with a loose rope and not too picky about the brand they drop it on. Had to leave the city a bit sudden-like, if you know what I mean. I'd aim to stay out of sight for a time and make some money while I did."

They all relaxed. "Ride with us if you like," the hardcase said. "Feller I know out there is calling in his friends – though I'd say it's guns he wants a mite more than ropes."

"I've guns at my belt," Duane said. "I'll

ride along and see what pay he offers for them. Call me Buck," he added.

"I'm Bart," the older man said. "Just Bart. And this here – " he grinned when he said it – "is the Jackrabbit Kid."

"I'm not," the boy said hotly. "Jack's my name, but that's all. You're too free with your tongue, Bart."

"And you're too lippy with your betters, Kid," Bart said. "You run like a jack and eat like a horse. Your ears droop and your mouth never shuts. Now what's that but a jackrabbit?"

The boy sputtered wordless anger.

Buck Duane knew the hot anger and the nameless pride that surged within the youngster and would shortly force him to reach for the holstered gun at his side. If he did that, Bart would probably kill him – not because he wanted to, but because a confrontation had taken place between two armed males and neither would be able to think of an alternative answer.

"It's a name," Duane said, "and not a bad one at that. You might say it's original. There must be a dozen Pecos Kids, but this one means you and nobody else."

The boy was diverted as Duane had intended he would be. "But – Jackrabbit," he said. "Who wants to be called for . . . ?"

"Lop-eared, mangy, cactus-jumping varmit?" Duane laughed. "I suppose that's what you were going to say. On the other hand the jack's not so bad. He can outrun a horse and kick a rattler to death and his females love him. He's mean when he wants, but he minds his own business – and he's so tough you have to hit himm with lightning to kill him. Not a bad name for a young man just starting out, I'd say."

Even Bart looked impressed. "By God, boy," he said, "I didn't rightly know what sort of handle I was putting to you. I surely didn't."

The young fellow was obviously pleased and mollified. "The way you put it stranger, it don't sound so bad after all. Has to be hit with lightning to kill him. I never really thought of it that way before. What's your handle, Mister?"

"Buck," Duane said. "Just you call me Buck."

"Don't you never learn, boy?" Bart reproved. "Out here you don't ask a man his name. Specially not a gunslinger."

The kid looked at Duane with new respect.

Shortly after dark they smothered the fire

149

and slept. It was summer, but each man put a blanket under him and slept fully dressed with his head on saddle or bedding roll and his weapons in easy reach.

Buck Duane lay on his back and saw the stars blaze like lanterns in the black immensity of sky above him. Far off a coyote yipped a call to its brothers, and rustlings in the grass told of mice and small creatures going to and fro. No larger animals moved so close to the smell of man and cooked food and fire except for their own horses. Duane knew when Bullet came to the stream to drink.

After a while he thought again of the name, "Jackrabbit Kid" and smiled. With that smile on his face he fell asleep.

They were up at daybreak and eating cold biscuit and meat. By instinct neither Bart nor Duane would risk a fire for coffee. They saddled and rode north all through that day along the bank of the stream.

Around four in the afternoon they came upon an old man camped by the trickle that the stream had become. He was a dirty old man with a tobacco-stained beard and an odor ranker than a spring-wakened bear.

His teeth were broken and snagged and one boot showed toes through a rent. His

150

only weapon was an ancient cap-and-ball buffalo gun with octagonal barrel and engraved lock plate. He called Bart by name and Bart called him Old Hank.

"Jerry left me here to p'int you fellers coming in," the ancient said importantly. "He's holding a herd by the spring in Old Comanche Draw. Ye're to lather them broncs going in, fer nobody late for the ruckus draws no pay."

Bart nodded. "I know the spot. How many has gone in, old Hairy Hank?"

The oldster ruffled. "Keep a civil tongue in your head, young Bart, er I'll tan your britches like I did yer daddy's long 'fore you was born. How should I know how many? This ain't the only road they riding in. You got any whiskey for an old man to warm his bones?" The question was directed to them all.

"I got no whiskey," Bart said. "Did I, I'd drink it myself."

"You want to trade for that gun?" Duane asked on impulse. "Might be I could find whiskey then."

The old man's face lit up at the thought until a dozen years dropped off his shoulders. "Whiskey? How much whiskey?"

"How much is it worth to you?" Duane asked.

The old man shook his head. "I feared you'd ask that. No, I can't trade, son. Leastways not my buffler gun. This here's the last I've got. The last of my manhood I mean. Why, with this gun, I could shoot the eye out of a gopher, and name you the eye to boot. Ag'in the Cheyenne once . . . " His voice trailed off.

Buck Duane found a flask with only an inch of whiskey in the bottom in his saddle bags, and gave it to the old man.

The three of them rode west and then a little north of west. Bart had been to the rendezvous before, and showed them the way. Duane memorized the landmarks as they rode. It was wild country, only recently ceded by the Indians and still sheltering occasional raiding bands of Comanche and Apache.

The plains rolled endlessly to a horizon broken in the west and south by jagged peaks and long blue ranges of hills unmapped and unnamed. Jagged ravines, hidden draws and valleys invisible until a rider reached the rim, scarred the earth as if a titanic jaguar had clawed and rent the land. A thousand wild blooms and twisted cacti sheltered in the grass, from sweet wild strawberry to the sacred mushrooms of the medicine men.

There were still buffalo to be seen, but in a few short years this would be cattle range from end to end. At least it would be, Buck Duane reminded himself, if missions like his own were not frustrated by the wild and merciless outlaws of the border.

About noon, while crossing an apparently unbroken plain, they apparently came to the rim of a vast sunken draw which stretched away a good six miles to the west. The gash was a hundred feet below the level of the plains and a trail wound down a short way from where they halted.

There was a shine of water in the valley and green shade of cottonwood. The grass stretched deep and green, and Duane could see cattle grazing and two separate horse herds, or remudas, watched by riders.

There were men at the head of the trail down into the valley, at least half a dozen of them sitting at ease below the rim of the drop-off. Bart rode ahead to parley with them briefly and then waved his companions to come on. They spurred their mounts to join him.

Duane studied these fellows carefully

without seeming to do so. It was always necessary for him to watch out for men who had known him during his outlaw days. The name of Buck Duane was a standing challenge to aspiring gunmen and established killers. To fight him and kill him would be a triumph that could make a man famous through the length and breadth of the West.

From long experience Duane knew that many would be unable to resist the challenge which he represented. He did not want to have to kill, but he wanted even less to fall before a backshooter's gun or that of a crazy kid inspired beyond his normal ability with a six-shooter.

He wanted even less to be recognized by someone who had known him as a Ranger. In that event every man in the valley would join in a crazy drive to shoot him down.

The outlaw, the killer, the gunman and the lawman alike lived only at the price of eternal vigilance.

Bart was similarly alert. The Kid was not. He rode with the careless innocence and friendly smile of a tail-wagging puppy.

Once down the narrow, winding trail to the valley floor they rode at once to the largest grove of cottonwoods. A rude corral of split sapplings had been fenced off here and there were three or four rudely constructed log cabins. Evidently this was a more or less permanent headquarters base for the rustlers. The first part of Buck Duane's mission had been accomplished. He'd located, and was about to join one of the bands Captain MacNelly had mentioned. The hardest and most dangerous work was still ahead.

Chapter III

When they had put their horses into the corral and their saddles and bedrolls outside the fence, one of the rustlers took the three riders to a cook shack where they were given big tin plates of beef and beans, biscuit with blackstrap molasses, and cups of strong boiled coffee. They ate with healthy appetite – most especially the Jackrabbit Kid.

After they had cleaned the plates a tall, dark man in a fringed buckskin jacket, tooled leather boots and Mexican silver spurs came out of what appeared to be the headquarters cabin and walked over to them. His hat was an oversized Mex sombrero and the leather of his gun belt and holster was elaborately worked. He wore a close-cropped beard – not stubble but carefully trimmed – and his eyes were curious light hazel shot with yellow like a cat's. Buck Duane knew him at once, but held his peace and gave no sign.

"My name's Jim Dancer," the man said.

"I captain the guns in this crowd. This is Jerry Link's company, but right now the hiring's for guns – and I do it. Any objection?"

Nobody said a word.

"We don't ask a man questions here," Dancer said. "You might say we hire the gun and don't care who pulls the trigger. Only one thing. You take my money – then you take orders from me. Any man who doesn't, I tend to personally. Until I tell you so, you'll be my man and nobody else's."

He paused again.

"Be sure that's understood. Now as to pay. You get a hundred dollars in United States gold coin today. After that you share in all the money that this band will make – and I can promise you that will be plenty. Jerry Link takes twenty per cent off the top, and I take fifteen. The rest is share and share alike."

He shook hands with each of the three. "Go on into the cabin for your gold," he said to Bart and the Kid. When Buck Duane started to follow he held him back.

"I know you," he said quietly.

Duane looked him in the face. "Hello, Jim. It's been a long time."

"So it has," Dancer said. "Six years at

157

least. I've been south of the Line most of that time. Your hired to me, Duane. How much will you be my man?"

Duane thought it over. "How do you mean that, Jim?"

"I can't tell you now." Dancer's face and manner were eager. "Something big in the wind, and I need men like you that I can trust. Walk away from the fire tonight. I'll find you and tell you then. If anything starts, look for me. There's plenty in it for you."

Duane just nodded, but kept a serene poker face. When Dancer left him, he walked on into the cabin after his two friends.

Jerry Link was inside, seated behind a table counting gold ten-dollar pieces out of a buckskin bag for Bart and the Kid. He looked up when Duane came through the door, and stopped what he was doing while he gave the Ranger a long looking over. Link could tell a real professional from a rough like Bart, and the new man interested him.

The rustler chief was a big man himself – as tall as Duane but broader and heavier. Men said he could straighten a horseshoe with his hands, and he looked it. His clothes were made by a San Antonio tailor. He was shaved and powdered as if a barber had been after him and there were pearl studs in the front of his not-overly-clean linen shirt.

His eyes were more intelligent than Bart's, but there was curiously strained quality about them. They were the eyes of the unscrupulous and successful businessman of all times and places.

"Hello," he said to the room in general, "now who is this?"

Duane just looked at him. "Call me Buck," he said.

"Call you Buck – George, Henry or Robert E. Lee," Jerry Link said. "I'll call you whatever you please, but I wish I knew who you are. You're not like the rest of these gunnies for sure. You're a man whose name I'd know if I heard it. I'll swear to that. You want to tell me?"

"Just Buck will do," Duane said.

"You must be real fast with that gun to take it so easy-like," Link said, with halfway challenge in his eye and voice.

Duane's face became an unmoving mask out of which the eyes looked bleakly. His right hand came to rest only an inch or so from the notched butt of the gun his father had worn before him. Deep inside him something cold and deadly came to life.

"There's just one way to find out,

159

Mister," he said so softly that his lips scarcely moved. Nonetheless, every man in the room heard the words and sensed the thing that spoke.

Jerry Link had no intention of fighting then. His face smiled broadly, though his eyes were cold. He kept both hands in sight and busy with the bag of gold coins on the table.

"Hold on," he said in a jovial tone. "No offense meant at all. Buck it is, as long as you say so. I'm here to hire men, not to quarrel with them."

Duane allowed the tension to hold just a second longer before he smiled and the whole roomful of men relaxed. Then he picked up his coins off the table and turned away.

Outside in the fresh air the Kid looked at him with a new respect. "I don't know who you are, Mister," he said impulsively, "and I'm not about to ask. That fellow in there was afraid of you. He didn't want it to show, but I could tell. You must be somebody like Doc Holliday or Curly Bill for him to be afraid. I'm proud to ride with you."

Duane looked at him. "A man should only be proud to ride with himself," he said.

"I can trust you, can't I?" the Kid asked.

Duane gave him a long, grave look. "Out here this side of the law," he said, "you mustn't ever take any man's word for that. You've got to make up your own mind to it. You have to learn to do that fast. You have to judge every man you let stand behind you."

"Well," the Kid said, "I trust you, Buck, whoever you are. This is all new to me. I was raised in Galveston on the Gulf of Mexico. I wouldn't be here except I killed a man." He saw Duane look at him. "Oh – not what you might think. It wasn't murder. He – insulted my sister. You understand I had to call him for that."

"I understand." Buck Duane's mind was back across the years to the boy that he had been. Again he buckled on his father's gun and walked downtown to seek a man. Again he saw a body in the dust.

He shook his head to drive the memories away. "It had to be, I suppose," he said, "but still I'm sorry, Jack." For fear or saying too much too soon, he walked away.

Men in the camp rested or drank or gambled through the afternoon. Before dusk another big meal was served and each man got a tin cup of coffee and whiskey – half and half. There was more liquor for those who wanted to pay for it. Voices rose until there was a rowdy clamor about the fires. These were desperate and reckless men, and there was tension in the air.

When darkness fell Duane walked away from the fires out to the edge of the grove on the side away from the corral. It wasn't long before he heard footsteps and made out Jim Dancer's figure coming towards him. The gunman had taken off his Mexican spurs and wore a low-crowned Stetson instead of the elaborate sombrero which he usually favored. In the darkness Duane recognized him mainly by the familiar tones of his voice.

"What's on your mind, Jim?" Duane asked.

"Give me time," Dancer said. "I won't say I wasn't surprised to see you here – but I will say I'm glad. I heard how you called Jerry's bluff, Buck, so I guess I won't have to explain to you the sort of man he is."

"Mean and cruel," Duane said. "Greedy above all, and sometimes too greedy to be smart."

"That's it," Dancer said. "That's purely it. Right now he's fixing to try something real stupid. He's going to tackle the Old Man himself – the rustler king – the one who makes the profits possible. He can't win, Buck. He can't."

"That all depends on how and what he does, don't it – Jim," Buck said in his usual mild tones.

"This time he's dead before he pulls trigger," Dancer said. "He and any ranny as sides him will be coyote bait this time tomorrow night."

"So soon?"

"And how do I know? That's what you're asking, Buck. The Old Man knows. Don't ask me how. He knows and he won't talk into no bushwhack any more than Tuanah Parker and his red devils would. I know he knows, and he'll cut Jerry Link to worm food all for sure. Him and those who hold close to him. I'm giving you the chance to step out of that. I'll not offer it again."

"You're asking me to side with you against Link and with this Old Man of yours," Buck Duane said. He heard a whisper of sound where a third man stood behind him to be sure he never left the spot alive unless he joined with Dancer.

"First tell your man behind me to go away, Jim," he said. "I don't have to draw. I've had a derringer in my left hand pointed at your belly since before you spoke first. It's a .44 rimfire, Jim. Your guts won't stand it."

Dancer grunted, and Duane heard the

163

man behind him walk away. "Don't worry, Jim," he said. "I'll join with you. This Link is nothing but a mouth to me."

"Then why the derringer?" Dancer said in relief.

"I just didn't want you to think any man could backshoot Buck Duane," the Ranger said. "I wanted you to remember just who I really am. It's best for us both that you do. Now I'll join with you in this fight. Not only that, but I'll speak for the two men who rode in with me today. Now tell me all you know and what you plan."

They talked for over an hour longer before going back into the grove to bed down for the night.

Chapter IV

Before dawn the camp was awake and the men moving according to Jerry Link's orders for the day. The rustlers who made up Link's original group were busy rounding up the herds of stolen cattle and horses and driving them up the hidden valley to its southwest end. Here there was a more gradual rise of land and another cleft in the walls through which stock could be driven up to the level of the plains.

The herds would be driven through this gap and over the plains to the west until intercepted by the drovers personally responsible to the 'Old Man,' who would take over the job. At this time also Jerry Link would be paid for the stolen stock at a rate previously agreed upon.

There was never any precisely appointed place of rendezvous. As Dancer had explained the night before. "That Old Man, he's a regular old gray wolf for smartness. If he named one spot to meet, somebody could lay an ambush there. So all he says is he'll meet on such and such a trail. You see?"

Jerry Link's plan was to attack the Old Man's band as soon as it appeared. For this purpose he infiltrated several of his hired gunmen among the drovers, trusting to the dust and confusion of a trail herd on the move to conceal their absence.

The rest of the gunmen, under the command of Jim Dancer, were to stay just over the rise of ground on the flank where the Old Man would not see them. At the first sound of shots they would ride in at a run to strike the enemy in flank and rear and complete their rout.

Strategically and tactically it was a good plan. The only fault lay in the fact that Dancer had sold out to the enemy before the first shot was to be fired. He had ten men with him, including Duane, Bart and the Kid, and all of them were in on the secret. On top of that, the main body of the Old Man's people were forewarned and on the alert.

Dancer kept his men much closer to the trail herd than had been originally planned. He saw the compact knot of strangers riding hard, not from the road ahead where Link expected them, but from the rear where they had watched the herd pass.

Caught by surprise, Link made a bold try. A spatter of rifle shots from his rearguard riders opened the battle. After that he could only fight.

The new riders came up with a whoop and stampeded the herd right through and over the Link riders. It was impossible to make a stand, and Link's men were run over or shot down in ones or twos almost before they knew what had hit them.

The hard knot of gunmen riding under the rustler's direct eye were another matter. Knowing they could expect no mercy, these fellows resolved to die hard. By desperate spurring about half of them got clear of the stampede just in time to find themselves in the path of Dancer's oncoming riders.

Someone in Dancer's party fired a shot and then both groups were galloping at each other like two Indian war bands, and firing as they came. Wounded horses screamed with pain. Men dropped the reins and slammed to the ground dead or wounded.

Duane held his fire. Gunman without equal as he was, he was still not a killer by preference. Link's riders were beaten. There was nothing to be gained by killing them, or by being killed by them in a senseless melee. If he could have spotted the rustler captain himself, it would have been another matter.

Link would remember the betrayal – and the name of every man involved. He would make it his business to hunt them down, and he'd remember the face of the mysterious 'Buck – just Buck.' As long as he lived, Link would represent a danger.

In the first wild charge, Duane did not see the rustler. Men from both bands fell. Others swept through. Duane whirled his horse in pursuit. It was then that he saw Link. The rustler had almost gotten away. About two hundred yards behind the fighting line his horse had broken its foreleg in an old gopher hole.

Link was on his feet, glaring wildly and defiantly around. His Winchester had been torn from his hand by the fall, but both ornately decorated .45s were still in their holster.

Buck Duane swung Bullet around, and at the same moment saw that the Kid had spotted Link. "Get back," Duane yelled. He was sure the inexperienced boy would get himself killed. The Kid didn't hear him, but Link did.

Duane swung out of the saddle and ran

forward on foot. "Fair fight!" he shouted. "Get back, Kid. This man's mine. Get back all of you. Fair fight and winner take all."

The other rustlers caught his meaning. He wanted a man-to-man shootout. If Link won, he'd go free. The idea appealed to their reckless minds. Two masters would meet and fight it out and a new legend of the owlhoot trail would be born.

To show his nerve, Duane swung Bullet's head so that when he dismounted he would have his back to the rustler for a few seconds. Ordinarily such a move would be suicide, and every man present knew it – but this was no longer a battle. For the two men it had become a ritual duel like the combat between Hector and Achilles under Trojan walls in the dim, barbaric past. If either man violated the unwritten frontier code, the watchers would shoot him down without mercy.

Buck Duane turned to face his enemy. They were on a level expanse of prairie overgrown with knee-high grass and surrounded by a rough circle of armed men. He and Link were about sixty yards apart. Neither would want to risk a shot at that distance.

Duane took the initiative at once by

starting a slow, implacable walk towards the rustler. All emotion had gone out of him except for the cold, terrible will to slay. This man must be killed, not for Duane's own sake, but for all that he and all the Rangers stood for in the world. Link was at once the enemy of Buck Duane and of all decent men and women everywhere.

To the watchers his walk might have seemed casual, but it was not. He was sure each lightly placed foot felt solid ground before he put his weight on it. His hands, which appeared to swing easily, were never more than an inch or two from the butts of his two guns. His eyes never wavered for an instant from the face of his enemy.

A lesser gunman might have watched his opponent's hands. Duane knew that the eyes would give first signal of the draw.

Closer and closer he came. He saw sweat burst and bead on the rustler's brow. He saw the man struggle to make himself walk forward in turn – and fail. Link's eyes became desperate.

In that precise instant, Duane knew himself the winner. He had won the battle to impose his strength on the other, and the thin, imponderable 'edge' that spelled victory was his.

Link braced his spread feet in the ground. To run was suicide. He had no choice but to stand and draw at the tall, spare figure which came remorselessly on.

Duane watched the rustler's face. He saw the lips skin back, the left eye close and the right bore suddenly at his face. Without hesitation his own hand dropped and gripped the notched butt of the .45 his father had worn. His thumb pulled the hammer back as the gun cleared leather. His trigger finger tightened and he fired precisely as the muzzle came level.

He never saw Link draw, but he heard the man's gun fire a split second behind his own. The shot sprayed dirt where it struck wild.

Duane's bullet struck Link exactly over the heart. The impact of the heavy slug was like a blow from a driven piledriver in force and effect. The man's arms and legs jerked wildly like those of a puppet. His body went back in a sort of awkward hop and then fell lifeless to the ground. Duane slid his own gun back into its holster and turned to walk back to the waiting Bullet.

He heard the wild yell of applause from the ring of sweating, dust-grimed men. He saw the Kid waving his hat and shouting with wide-open mouth. He felt a little sick.

By the time Duane was halfway to his horse, he was surrounded by a respectful ring of rustlers and outlaws. They'd seen – and so been part of – a shootout that would be remembered as long as men rode the West, and they knew it.

"I never saw his hand move," one man said. "I swear I never even saw him draw. It was like the bullet came from the palm of his hand. That's what it was."

"That Link was fast," another said. "I seen him kill three men myself, but against this one he was like a child with a toy gun. He never had a chance."

"My Lord, Buck," Jim Dancer called out. "That was the finest draw I ever saw – bar none. The finest and the smoothest."

"You know him?" said a voice. "Who is he?" Others echoed the question.

Dancer hesitated. "Hold on boys. He might not want to say. Ask and see if he'll tell you.

"He'll tell me," said a new voice quietly, and a rider brought his horse into the center of the ring.

Duane knew the tone of deserved command when he heard it. He turned slowly and found he had to look up at the man who sat a big gray stallion with the ease and flair of another J.E.B. Stuart. He wore a plain black suit, a theatrical black cloak and a broad-rimmed black hat that looked as if it ought to sport a plume, but didn't. His boots were unornamented but of the finest leather. He wore one gun, belted high under his long cloak and black coat. It wasn't a quick-draw rig.

There was no doubt at all that this was the legendary Old Man, the king of the badlands outlaws. His face and manner showed command in spite of the white hair and smooth cheeks of age. His blue eyes were restless in the calm face, but they looked down at Duane without fear or hesitation.

"You'll tell me your name," he said in statement and not in question.

"I will," Duane said without hesitation. Then he let it drop. He let suspense build until the men about him were quiet and held their horses still – until he and the Old Man were alone in a circle of waiting and of silence. Then: "I'm Buck Duane."

"I thought so," the Old Man said. "I saw your father kill a man with that same style."

It was impossible to tell whether the Old Man was speaking truly, but the very statement gave him standing with his men. It restored the balance Duane had moved

173

with his announcement. Duane's respect for the ability and intelligence of this man increased.

"Ride out a ways with me," the outlaw said. "I'd like to talk with you, Buck."

They rode to the top of a small rise in the prairie where Bullet and the gray could graze side by side and where the outlaw chief could watch everything that went on.

The fighting was ended and men were busy rounding up and bringing back the stampeded beasts. The bodies of the dead were left unburied on the ground to be eaten by wolf and coyote or by the buzzards circling overhead.

The Ranger hoped, in the back of his mind, that the Kid noticed the bodies. It was a careless and disreputable end to a dozen outlaw trails that had begun as human lives. These had been men – and their fellows left them for meat to feed the big, stinking birds. They were as unmissed and unmourned as so many lizards trampled by the horses.

"You're thinking," the Old Man said. "It's not a usual thing for a man to do out here."

"Sometimes I forget myself," Duane said.

"You're not a usual man, Buck," the outlaw said. "You don't have to pretend with me. I know a fine sense of the dramatic when I see one. I am where I am and what I am today, Mr. Duane, because I have a natural and cultivated gift for reading men as others read books. Now there's a riddle I must read from you – the riddle of just what you are doing here."

Duane hesitated, searching his mind for the right answer to give this strange old man.

"Oh, I know in general why you're with these people," the Old Man said. "A man of your sort is forever on the run in the very nature of things. What I want is a good deal more specific than that. Why with Link's band instead of any other? Why did you side with me instead of with Link at the showdown? And finally why that dramatic duel back there? Much may depend on your answers, Buck." The frost-cold eyes fixed on the Ranger.

Duane looked him right in the eye. "That's a lot of questions, sir. I'll try to give you honest answers – not because I fear you, but because it's my nature. Actually one phrase will answer most of what you asked. I wanted to meet you and work for you – to ride with you, that is. I sought out Link because I heard he sold to you. It was pure luck I heard of his intentions. Jim Dancer knew men and wanted me on his side. I joined because it gave me a reason to ask to stay with you – and because I never for a minute thought Link could beat you."

The Old Man was smiling. "You tell a good story, Duane; but what about the killing of Link? Was that for me, too?"

"I wouldn't pretend to you it was only that," Duane said. "It was better for Jerry Link to die than to live and hate me and perhaps strike me in the future. That was part of it. It was a chance to win the respect of you and your men. That was another part."

He didn't mention his third reason – the desire to keep Link from killing the Jackrabbit Kid. The Old Man might understand that reason, but he was unlikely to respect it. More likely he would count it a sign of weakness in Duane.

The outlaw had been looking out over the plains. Now he turned back to Duane. "I believe you," he said. "You speak well. I've lost some men in this fight in spite of the outcome never being in doubt. I'll need to replace them. You can be one of those to ride with me. In fact, you and Dancer can pick the others. I'll be glad to have you with me, Buck."

"Thank you," Duane said.

The second major step of his mission had been accomplished just as Captain MacNelly had foreseen that it would be. The hardest part was still ahead.

Chapter V

Once in control of the field, the outlaws moved with a speed and businesslike precision which put to shame the effort's of Jerry Link's men. Cattle and horses which had stampeded over miles of prairie were rounded up and brought back at a fast clip. They were then split again into a total of four smaller herds which could each be managed by a few riders.

The first of these trail herds moved out as soon as it had been formed. The others were each only an hour or so behind. To avoid the later groups finding scant forage, the herds did not follow in each other's tracks but fanned out on roughly parallel routes. A rear guard of picked gunmen stayed behind to detect and deal with any possible pursuit either by a posse or an Indian band which might have picked up the trail.

If pursuit had materiliazed, a single rider could have alerted the nearest herd which, in turn, would warn the others. By day a signal fire could do the job instead of a rider. Meanwhile the attacker would be ambushed by some of the most deadly fighters in the West.

Buck Duane found himself held with this picked cadre of gunfighters. It was a compliment, for these were all hardened frontier guerilla fighters and gunslingers, and it kept him out of the dust and confusion of the herds – not to speak of the work of driving, feeding and herding cattle and horses.

On the other hand, it cut him off from contact with his only possible allies and friends. After the shooting of Jerry Link, Bart and the Jackrabbit Kid had attached themselves to Duane. They shared in the prestige of having ridden into camp with him, felt unbounded confidence in his skill with revolver, and firmly proclaimed themselves his friends and followers. Both had, however, been assigned to go with the second of the four trail herds.

Jim Dancer, who might have sided Duane if he felt it to be his own advantage, had been assigned as captain of the third of the four herds.

Each of these smaller units was handled by a captain who answered directly to the

Old Man and six riders. Unlike a regular trail herd, there were no regular cooks or horse herders with these groups. The outlaws took turns at these jobs, and Buck Duane was sure that even a coyote would turn up his nose at some of the resultant meals. There was plenty of food, though no chuck wagons. Flour and other supplies move on pack horses.

The Chief's picked group fared otherwise, and much to their advantage. Besides the Old Man himself there were nine gunslingers, of whom Duane was one. In addition there were two big tough men. After the first day Duane assumed they had been personal bodyguards to the Chief back in the East. At least they were blindly loyal to him, and to him alone. One served as cook, producing menus that included such luxuries as canned corn, tomatoes and peaches as well as a glass of whiskey for each man. The other was a horse wrangler and herded the remuda of spare mounts.

After a week of generally westerly movement, the habitual caution of the rear guard was considerably relaxed. They were now a couple of hundred miles from the nearest really settled country in which a sizable posse could have been raised and far beyond even an outlying ranch. No one came this way but Indians and men of their own stripe or an occasional lonely trapper. They kept an eye out, of course. It would have been impossible for such men not to have done so, but there was no real expectation of danger.

About noon of the eighth day the trail of the herds they had been following all turned due south insted of west. It was the first indication the Ranger had had of the direction in which their market really lay. No one had talked around the camp fires, and he hadn't dared ask any questions.

Their route so far had skirted the southern limits of the wild and empty Llano Estacado. Now it turned south and headed towards the spot where the town of Marathon, Texas, would one day be built. The land began to rise through a tangle of rugged hills and gorges.

Ahead of them Duane saw the looming ridges of what he knew must be the Santiago Mountains. He'd heard of this country in his outlaw days, though never riding this far himself. It was reputed to be savage country, 'Man-killer mountains and wild beasts to eat your bones.' If there were safe passes through, he hadn't heard of them, although the outlaw grapevine of hunted men would usually pass along all such information.

The Old Man seemed to know where he was going, however.

On the first day after the turn south he called together Duane and two of the other riders. Both of them were men making their first trip with him.

"Take a spare horse apiece and load a pack horse with four days' rations," he ordered. "We're making a special run ahead of everybody. The herds and the rest of your fellows will catch up to us at rendezvous."

The four of them circled the herds and went slightly west of south at a pace that brought out the best in their horses. The Chief kept in the lead. To Duane there was no trace of a trail, let alone a road, but the man went as surely and as steadily as if following a heavily traveled turnpike. It was obvious that he'd been this way many times before.

They rode straight for the mountains which reared an apparently unbroken wall. From a distance the mountains were purple spires marching together as if to bar mankind forever from some secret treasure to the south.

"We ain't going over them things," a rider

called Louman said incredulously. "One of them old mountain men like Jim Bridger would be hard put to do it on foot, let alone man and horse. For a herd of beef critters, it'd be purely impossible."

The Old Man reined to a halt and spoke to them all. "For the first and last time I'm telling you," he said. "Whatever I ask you to do is possible. We don't climb those mountains – though I think it might be done. There's a pass only I and the Indians know, Persimmon Gap I call it, because there's wild fruit growing there. Fruit and sweet water and an easy grade to take the steers across. We'll camp there in the morning at as pretty a spot as ever one of you has seen. That's where we meet the guide who'll take us the rest of the way."

"The rest of the way?" one of the men asked. "Where's that?"

The Chief was in a good humor. Instead of letting his temper rise, he just chuckled. "You ask no fool questions," he said, "and I won't have to give fool answers. Where we go is nobody's business but mine just so long as I take you there and bring you back with your pockets full of heavy gold eagles.

"Now is it? Of course not. So all I'll say is we go through some of the worst country

Satan ever made as slick as a hot knife cutting butter. We go places nobody on earth could follow us, and we ride easy all the way."

"It sound okay to me, Chief."

"It had better, boy. It just had better."

"Is this guide one of yours?" That was Louman.

The Chief pondered. "You'll have to know soon or late, so best I tell you now. Our guide is nobody's man – matter of fact, no man at all. To be honest she's a woman. Not only that but a young and handsome woman – and a lady, if any of you know what that is."

Buck Duane and the other two looked their incredulity.

"You'll see," the Old Man said with satisfaction. "Just one thing, though. I tell it so you remember. I said this is a lady. No man of mine can put hand to her – not the tip of a finger nor the breath of a word from his mouth. She's to be as safe in this crew as an angel in heaven. There'll be no whiskey issued while she rides with us. No chancy talk. No gambling round the fires at night. The men will wash, and call her Ma'am. Whoever breaks the rules I'll kill myself."

"What's so holy about this one? Ain't a woman a woman?"

"If you could understand the answer to that," the outlaw said, "you wouldn't have to ask the question. Two reasons, then. She's the guide. If she rides away we're lost – every man jack of us. And if we could find a way out, she's got friends in those mountains to see that we don't."

"Comanches?" Buck Duane asked.

The chief nodded. "And Apaches, boys. Crueller than buzzards and deadlier than snakes. Men who'd eat us for the salt in our meat. We'll be watched every step past the Gap, and if they turn hostile not even a memory of us will ever get out of here."

After that the men rode wrapped in their own thoughts. Duane was particularly busy trying to think out the mystery. A woman who knew this country and was guarded by the wild Indians of the mountains had to be an Indian herself, or somebody who lived with the tribes.

Yet the Chief has used the word 'lady' and had obviously used it in the sense with which he'd been familiar in his original home. Duane had decided some time earlier that the outlaw had to be a product of the old pre-war Cotton South. Men of that stripe used 'lady' in a special connotation that meant far more than 'female' or 'woman.'

It was obvious also that this lady guide was the key to answer all the questions which had baffled Captain MacNelly and the Rangers. The stolen herds disappeared from sight of lawmen because they went through country considered absolutely impassable by the frontiersmen, and accordingly unknown to them. They could do so only because there was a guide available.

On the other hand the stolen stock couldn't stay in such a wilderness. Roving bands of Stone Age savages don't buy beef for gold. Somewhere or other the ponies and beeves had to come out again. At the end of this trip, if all went well, he'd know where and how. He already had one invaluable fact. Persimmon Gap was on Texas soil. A few Rangers could ambush the future herds there. Of course there were probably other passes going south. Without knowledge of the final destination, nothing could really be accomplished.

He'd hoped that by joining the band he'd overhear enough talk from the men to find out what he had to know. The Old Man had proved smarter than he thought. Apparently only he – and possibly a few trusted lieutenants – knew where they were going. The rest just rode where they were told. The men who knew the truth kept closed mouths.

There was no help for it. Duane had to go every step of the way with his band. He tried to think what he'd heard about the territory they were headed for. There had been vague talk of a range of mountains. The Chisos, he thought they were called. "Peaks that would kill a curly horn sheep," an old mountain trapper had said. "No roads, no water, no buffler, no beaver. Just rock all the way into the clouds. Nothing lives there. Even the buzzards don't fly over. They'd starve on them hills."

It wasn't an encouraging prospect. However, the old trappers were notorious for embroidering every tale. If the country was really that bad, no herd could get through – and the Chief had used this route often, by the way he talked. Well, he'd soon find out what sort of lady came from country 'that would starve any buzzard.'

The campsite at the entrance to Persimmon Gap was everything the Chief had promised – ripe fruit, sweet water, grass and trees. The men, including Duane, ate heartily and slept well.

In the morning, when Duane opened his eyes, the guide had come into camp so silently as not to awaken any of the men. She was drinking coffee by the fire with the Chief.

The first impression Duane got was a slender, rounded female body seen from the rear. She was dressed in buckskin jacket and loose trousers that at once concealed and revealed her womanhood. Her hair was bound round by a blue silk kerchief, but raven locks escaped at the neck and over the ears. Her back was towards him and they were talking in voices too low to overhear.

A little to her right and rear and old Apache squatted on his heels. At first sight he was a bundle of filthy, shapeless rags gripping an ancient double-barreled Hawken-made buffalo gun in one brown claw. He had heard the slight sounds Duane made on waking, and was regarding the Ranger out of beady black eyes. The rest of his face was hidden by loose rags hanging from the filthy turban that both concealed and protected his ancient head.

Eyes bluer than a summer sky met Buck Duane's. He saw youth and warmth and the

188

pink of blood under sunbrowned cheeks. He saw white teeth and a high, broad brow and a firm, determined chin above the soft white column of throat. There was a spark of something intangible that leaped between them and needed no words.

Then: "Good morning, rider," she said. "Come and have some coffee with us."

Chapter VI

It was two days more before the first of the trail herds reached Persimmon Gap. The others were right on its heels. The riders rested another day before any attempt was made to push on. The beasts were rested, fed and watered, to be ready for what all believed would be the difficult stretch ahead.

In those days Buck Duane was constantly near Juana – it was the only name she gave. The Old Man had taken him aside the first morning.

"Seems like she's taken a shine to you, Duane," he'd said. "You stay right close to her. I can't exactly appoint you Captain of the Royal Guard, so to speak, but you stay just as close as if that's what I'd done. She fears nobody – and that old Indian is supposed to be her guard. You know what that amounts to. There's men here would sooner backshoot an Apache than spit. There's others too stupid not to take the girl into the trees by force if they had to. I don't have to tell you what men will do to a girl out here."

"No," Duane said, "you don't. Anybody tries it, I'll stop him."

"You do it boy. You do just that. Anything happens to that girl, we're all dead – every man of us. Dead and our skulls bleaching on a stick outside a 'Pache hogan. There's men up there – " he gestured vaguely to the south – "that worship the ground she walks on."

"I'll manage," Duane said. "I'll remember."

"See that you do. Kill a man if you have to, but I misdoubt you will. They saw you bring down Jerry Link and I don't reckon there's a man here to face you lessen he's drunk or crazy. If you have to shoot one, though, I'll back you all the way. My word on it, Buck."

Duane was sure that he meant it.

Staying close to the girl kept him busy. She insisted on inspecting every head of stock that was driven into camp, to 'make sure that it can stand the drive.' She spoke to the men of the need to stay close to the herd, not straggle, and leave all decisions to the Old Man and herself.

"Mind your own business if you want to get through alive," she told each group in turn. "If you see anything being stolen – even your own saddle, mind – you come tell me. It will be returned. If you go after the thief, somebody will be hurt and maybe even a war started."

"I ain't afraid of no Injuns," one rider had growled under his breath.

Juana heard, and turned on him with eyes blazing. "Then you're a fool, rider," she said. "Then you're a simple fool. There's proud and deadly men watching this herd and every man and beast in it all the way. The tribes in there fear nothing – and with cause. Offend them, and they'll swallow every man and beast of you like a ripe persimmon off the tree there."

The outlaw only spat. Buck Duane moved a step forward. "Take your hat off when you talk to a lady," he said.

That brought the rough up short. Duane's voice was gentle – but it had been just as gentle when he spoke to Jerry Link. The rider lowered his eyes and took off his wide-brimmed hat.

"That's better," Duane said easily. "Now listen, all of you. Any man don't heed what Miss Juana says to him, had better hope the warriors get to him before me and the Old Man do. They'll be ministering angels compared to what the Chief will do to him, and every man can bet on that."

There was no more open defiance.

Now that all the herds were reunited, Bart and the Kid had once more attached themselves to Duane. The three of them shared a campfire and put down their bedrolls together close to Juana's own camp. In this way one or the other of them was always awake and alert to guard against danger to her.

During the day the old Indian, whom she called Poco – Spanish for little man – was always at her heels. At night he melted into the dark, but Duane was sure he was never far away. The old Apache did not seem a very formidable guard. Even the top of his turban only reached to a height of five feet two, and he looked like nothing more than an ambulatory bundle of rags with two black eyes peering out.

Duane knew better. A man like this would have developed incredible endurance and cunning. "He can walk an antelope till it dies of weariness, steal the food from a wolf's mouth, and hide behind a blade of grass," Buck Duane told the Kid. "That gun of his is a Hawken, one of the most accurate ever made. It throws a two-ounce slug that'll paralyze a charging buffalo, and he can hit a sparrow with it as far as he can see one. What you think is a poor old man, Kid, is more like a one-man army – and don't you ever forget it."

The Kid only nodded. These were rough days for him. He was torn between an adolescent passion for Juana and a chivalrous resolve to respect what he obviously considered to be Duane's prior right to her. Duane knew how he felt, but there was nothing to say that wouldn't just make him feel worse.

The more Duane watched the boy, the more he saw his own youth over again and the more he regretted the Kid's presence in the camp. This was an outlaw band.

The men who made it up could never again return to the civilized world behind the frontier. Their lives were as certain as those of the inarticulate wild beasts with which they shared the wastelands of the outer frontier.

They had no pasts to be proud of, no futures to look forward to. Each night's lonely fire might be the last to warm their bones. They lived in fear and rage and unspoken loneliness, and they died by violence to the thunder of guns or the swift jerking of a hangman's noose.

He tried to point this out to the boy more than once, but without success.

"I killed a man," the Jackrabbit Kid said with a stubborn set to his jaw. "Whether or not I like it I can't go back. I can't let them hang me. I don't have any choice. I'm an outlaw just like you are, Buck."

It was the last sentence that twisted into Duane just like a knife. The boy wanted to be like him – or rather like what he believed Duane to be. In his friend he saw the model of the gunman, the calm and deadly slayer of men, the hero of the bank. Duane could not reveal the truth without jeopardizing his whole mission and breaking his faith as a Texas Ranger.

Juana saw the struggle within him and divined its basis. "The Kid is a good boy," she said one day. "I don't think he'll stay with these men or become like them. The West is wide. In California they will not know what he has done or care. He can go there and make a life."

"You know California?" Duane was surprised.

She laughed a delighted golden laugh. "I

195

went to school there for years. Surely, Buck, you didn't think Poco taught me to speak English! You can't have thought I was only a mountain Indian girl? They don't read and write, you know. They don't lead men or wear a revolver as I do."

She paused for a moment. "Some of them are very lovely, though, Buck. Perhaps there are times when I envy Poco's granddaughters the simplicity of the lives they live."

"Who . . . ?" Buck Duane began and hesitated.

"Who am I? What am I doing here? Don't ask me now, Buck. There's a secret, but it isn't mine to give away. Not now it isn't. I've taken an oath – a very solemn oath. My lips are sealed."

She looked at him with mute appeal, her face more serious than he had ever seen it.

"I understand," Duane said. "At least I do about the oath. I've taken one, too, about some things. I want to know about you, Juana, but I won't press you now or ever till you're ready to tell me yourself of your own free will."

They stood together looking down the length of the meadow where the stolen horses had been gathered. Beyond were clean, high, sweeping curves of the mountains.

He looked at her and saw her breasts like the hills and the wind blowing strands of raven hair about her cheeks. He saw the long, sweet oval of her face and the incredibly blue eyes like chips of lapis lazuli, and a feeling he had thought long lost rose up within him.

She smiled a special smile for him. "Thank you, dear Buck," she said.

The Old Man called Duane to his fire that night to talk to him alone. He poured himself a shot of whiskey in the silver cap of a leather-bound flask. Then he poured again and handed the cap to Duane.

Duane sniffed the whiskey appreciatively and then emptied the small silver cup into the fire. The flames bit the alcohol and danced a blue flicker where it fell.

"You made a rule," he told the Chief. "You can break it for yourself, but I can't. No drinking in this camp, you said."

"I knew it," the outlaw said. "I knew it from the first."

He waited for Duane to answer, but the Ranger only sat quietly. Experience had taught him not to talk when another man was probing or testing him. When someone tried to look into his mind it was better to say as little as possible.

"You're no more a run-of-the-mill thief and scoundrel than I am," the Chief said at last. "There's few can equal you with a gun. I've seen them all, and if you're not the best, the best is still not safe from you. Yet you're not a killer for the love of it. I know you're an outlaw, but something inside tells me you don't fit the role. What are you, Buck Duane?"

"I'm your hired gun."

The Old Man moved in anger. He wore his long, black old-fashioned frock coat buttoned around him against the evening chill, but under it Duane could see a clean linen shirt with golden studs. The Old Man's hands were clean and almost frail but somehow cruel like the claws of a hawk.

"Duane . . . Duane," he said at last, "I'd like to be your friend, but how can I when you make sport of me?"

Buck Duane still sat silent.

"When I was your age," the Chief said, "I owned broad acres in the Delta and five hundred slaves. I had a great white house and women, white or black, for every night in the year. I rode with Nathan Forrest before I commanded a rabble like this. I drank my whiskey from cut crystal, and I shall again. A man like you could go a long way in my service."

"I mean to do just that," Duane said.

"Good. Good. I'd hoped you'd say just that. But remember, Duane, and don't make sport of me. Don't mock me and don't betray me. Don't try to play your hand and mine. We play my hand and it's good enough to win for us all. I do the thinking, Mr. Duane, and all is well."

Duane gave him a long, level look across the fire. "You have a particular point in mind, of course."

"You see that, do you?" The outlaw brushed a hand across his shaggy white eyebrows. "It's the girl. The Indian Queen." He laughed. "It's Juana. I put you to guard her and she likes you. She'll have no one else. But she's not yours, Duane. She's mine. Oh, I don't mean to bed with. I'm old for that. Take her into the bushes if you like and she'll go . . . but never forget she's mine to guide my herds. Don't ask her to guide for you, or you're dead and your bones white, man.

"And don't look at me with your frosty eyes. I'm no Jerry Link to stand against you on the open prairie with fifty fools to gape.

I've forty men to shoot you in the back. I've a cook to slip death in your coffee cup. Cross me, Duane, and you won't ever have a second chance."

"Now hold on," Duane said. "If I was the man you picture there you'd be dead by now. Or I could kill you where we sit. Oh, I know your bodyguards are out there in the dark with buckshot loads to cut me down. They'd never see my hand move or know a thing till you fell forward and the fire burned off your beard."

"And so?" The outlaw chief was calm enough.

"I'm your man." Duane said, "but never from fear. You've got something here that a man has to have if he wants to go out of the badlands. The name of it is Organization. I need it and can't make it for myself, because I never ran a plantation or commanded a regiment. As long as you have that you can turn your back to me as safe as if you had a sheet of steel under that fancy coat of yours."

It was a long gamble, and Buck Duane realized it perfectly well. He'd revealed himself as a thinking man, and if the Chief didn't believe in his loyalty, he was marked for death. No outlaw captain dares to tolerate a thinking man in the band unless he can be absolutely sure of his loyalty.

They sat for a time and watched the fire. Then the Chief took two cigars from the silver case and offered one to Duane. "Light up," he said. "I made no rule about these. I'm glad we talked man. I could tell there was something in your mind that made you different from the rest of them out there. Some of them are herd dogs and some are fighting pit bulls, but you, Duane, you're a man. Not only a man but a thinking man."

"Thank you," Duane said. "You're a thinking man yourself."

"Both of us know the key to success is this business," the Chief went on as if he hadn't heard. "It has to be organized. I set up my market first. I can pay the rustlers better than any market near to them. I handle stock in wholesale lots, as a merchant would say. I have a market and I have a way to reach that market where I can't be followed."

"Do you really need the girl?" Duane asked.

"You mean why don't I just drive through by myself?" the outlaw said. "You're a thinker, man. You tell me."

"Because she keeps the Indians off you?"

"That's one reason. Maybe it's the biggest

one. I don't know how many Indians there are out there or how well armed. Still, I can't risk being cut off in those mountains.

"The other reason is she never guides us by exactly the same route. As many times as I've been through I can't be absolutely sure I could make it on my own. You'll see for yourself shortly. Well now, Mister Buck Duane, do you want to be my man?"

This time Duane didn't hesitate in his answer. "Yes, I do. I'd be a fool not to hold to a man who can do what you're doing."

"You'll not regret it. I'm generous to my men. You'll live well and die in your bed in a mansion looking down on whatever city you choose. You'll have children to mourn you and a bishop to pray over your tomb. Believe me, man, I can make you rich and I will because I need men like you as much as you need me. Now go on back and find some sleep. We move out in the morning."

Duane lay in his blankets that night and thought of his talk with the Chief. Above him the stars blazed like lamps in the clear air as they swung their magnificent slow minuet about the sleeping earth. The air he breathed came clear and cold over thousands of miles of prairie and mountain and bore with it all the life essence of that journey. He could sense the slow breathing of a million sleeping buffalo and the quickened heartbeats of gopher and mouse and small scurrying creatures.

He knew the hunger of the questing lobo wolf and the exaltation of the mountain goat looking down over hundreds of miles of moon-washed foothill and plain. In the wind he smelled pine and oak and cottonwood and the acrid mesaquite. For a moment he was part of the land and the land was part of him.

It was all of this that he was being asked to sell for a promise of gold and women and a fever of greed. He thought of the Old Man in his broadcloth coat and linen shirt, his diamond rings and hidden derringer. He thought of the mind twisted by greed for gold and power, and by the endless fear that walked in the shadows of both.

He thought – but he did not envy the Chief.

Chapter VII

The long column of men and beasts got under way in the clear, chill light of the next morning's dawn with a great sound of hoofs and rattling horns, and lowing of cattle and the neigh and whinning of hundreds of horses, and the shouts and whoops of the rustlers as they started the herd. This time they were going through as a single herd – all under the control of the mysterious girl who had ridden in out of nowhere.

Juana and the Old Man, with Buck Duane and a half dozen of the gunslingers, rode point to show the way and keep out of the dust and confusion of the herds.

The girl's horse was a magnificent beast of a breed which Duane had never seen before. Its body was a shimmering color just off true gold while the flowing mane and tail shone silver white in the sun. She had told him it was called a palomino and was bred by the haughty Mexican landholders in the southern part of California. It was a spirited animal, much given to prancing and the caracole, and Juana was a beautiful and inspiring sight as she headed the long column up the pass.

The pace was easy. The Chief wanted to bring every beast to market in prime condition so that it would bring a higher price. Besides, with no remaining danger of pursuit, there was no real reason to hurry.

They came over the spine of the pass late on the following day and had their first glimpse of the country to the south through which the drive must go. Directly ahead, at a distance of about thirty miles, they saw the looming bulk of the Chisos Mountains rising like a monumental blue-green pyramid against the clear blue sky.

From that distance they seemed to be piled arrows of naked rock, though the outlines were softened and the peaks blanketed by more than a thousand varieties of growing plant from the spined, scarlet-bloomed strawberry cactus of the flats to ancient, wind-twisted Douglas fir at the peaks.

The flat plain under the mountain loom looked unbroken – but this was illusion. Unseen to the watchers, arroyos and steep canyons, many of them awesomely deep, slashed the sands and gave a home to mule deer, cougar, and other beasts. Antelope flashed their white rumps as they bounded away across the plains, and rattlesnakes and lizards uncounted sheltered from the heat under cactus or piled stone.

Some miles ahead and a little to their left a line of green from tree and brush showed the presence of water – the nameless stream that men would later call Tornillo Creek. It skirted the hills and poured its water down to empty in the Rio Grande.

At first Buck Duane thought that this must be the route they would take. An easy drive, he thought. Follow that creek and push the herds across to Mexico. Buyers could wait safely on the other side.

He realized then that this would be far too easy. It didn't check out at all with the need for a guide or with the elaborate preparations already made for crossing the roughest sort of country. More than that, it was sure that the entry of large herds into Mexico at this point would be known to the government officials there and they would have passed along the information to the Texas authorities and so to Captain MacNelly.

Sure enough, the drive stopped at the

headwaters of the creek just long enough to rest and water the stock, and make an overnight camp.

At this point two bands of Indians came into camp under safeguard promised by the Chief. Apparently one was composed of Apaches and the second and larger group of Comanches. There was a ceremonial pow-wow with the Old Man and Juana in the evening with feasting, pipe smoking and speeches. In the morning each band was allowed to cut out a small herd of cattle and horses and drive it away. By an hour after dawn they were gone.

"What does it mean?" the Jackrabbit Kid asked Duane. "I thought all Indians out this far were hostiles."

"They are," Duane told him. "You can bet your hair on it. If anyone of those jolly riders out there caught you alone this side of the pass, he'd bushwhack you before you knew it. This is where the Old Man pays them off for safe passage through the rest of their country. If he didn't they'd be killing riders and stealing stock every foot of the way from here on out. Believe me, it's a lot safer and cheaper to do it this way."

"Miss Juana lives with them?" the Kid asked again. "I don't understand it. She's so sweet and all and like a lady from back home."

The Kid sensed the tension back of that answer and decided to change the subject. "Watch this draw," he said. "I been practicing. Ain't it good?" His hand flashed down to pull the big gun out of its holster.

"It's a good draw," Duane said, "for an East Texas kid your age. That's all. It's fast, but not sure. You couldn't do it like that with a stampede coming up behind and your pony going end over end from fright. You couldn't do it with a man in front and one off to your left both drawing on you at once. You're a showman with that gun, Kid. Out here that's not enough. You have to be better than that."

"I practice every day," the Kid said. "How long before I'll be good enough?"

"Never," Duane said, "Before you're good enough with that thing you'll be dead. You'll go up against a killer, boy, and that'll be it. You'll be a trick shot and an artist with the gun and a real killer will cut you down while you're still making up your mind to draw. It's not speed that gives a man the edge, or skill or fancy shots. The thing that means the edge is the desire to kill. The man who has it'll get you every time."

The Kid's face fell. He scuffed the sand with one boot toe in dejection.

"Don't take it that way, Kid," Duane said. "Outside of killing, the real gunman isn't worth a damn. He just goes on killing and killing until somebody a little better or a little luckier kills him. He never sleeps more than minutes at a time and never twice in the same place for fear of being killed. He puts his back to the wall all his life because he can't trust anyone he sees. He eats wild meat without salt and drinks alkali water and he's never clean because sand isn't soap. If he dies in the open air nobody bothers to bury him.

"You can go home. You have it in you to be a real man and walk the streets with your head up. You can make a life like a man and not like a lobo skulking on the high plains. Don't you see that, boy?"

"But Buck, if all that's really so . . . ? I mean, why didn't you? I mean – you are a gunslinger, aren't you?"

It was an unforgivable question, and the Kid realized it almost at once. His face reddened with embarrassment and regret.

Duane didn't respond with anger. "Suppose I told you, Kid," he said, "that when I needed somebody to talk to me like I

209

just did to you he wasn't there? Suppose I said I thought I was trapped with no way out until after a while I really was? Sometimes a man gets a chance to make a choice just once. If he misses that chance, it may never come again."

It wasn't the whole truth about Buck Duane, but it was close enough. It was all he could say.

The herd moved out again the next morning, moving just to the east of the foothills of the Chisos mountains. It was far from a straight route, as frequent detours around the deep arroyos had to be made as well as bends to bring the beasts past the comparatively few supplies of clean water.

After two days Juana, in response to some sign known only to herself, ordered a turn due west. This aimed them right at the highest and loftiest peaks of the mountains.

As soon as the herd straightened out on this new route, Duane could see smoke signals rising in the highest peaks ahead. The Old Man saw it too, and questioned Juana.

"Don't worry," she told him. "Those are Apache fires. They're made by Poco's people. They just give the news of our

210

coming and the word that we come in peace."

Later, when they were riding alone, she told Buck, "In the raiding days – not so long past at that – the Apaches lived in the high mountains. The Comanches were the stronger tribe and held the plains where we ride now. Comanche war bands going into Mexico to raid or to sell Texas booty circled the mountains to the east or west. Sometimes the tribes were at war and there were desperate battles. Usually the Apaches would try to cut off a Comanche party who had finished a raid and had guns, prisoners or horses with them. Sometimes they won. That's how Poco got his gun."

"You seem to be equally at home with both tribes," Duane said.

"I am," she admitted. "I have good friends among both and can go and come perfectly freely. They will not harm me." She sensed the intensity of his unspoken curiosity and added with a smile, "I'll tell you why. It's because I never tell the secrets of one tribe to the other. Because of that they both trust me. Besides, I bring presents to my friends, and I arrange for this outlaw we ride with to pay for his passage in meat and in trade goods that they need."

"Including guns?" Duane asked bitterly.

"Of course," she said. "These people must hunt and defend themselves just like anybody else. Just like your Texans do. These tribes don't go out to raid any more since the army posts were built north and west of them. If an American is ever killed with those guns, it's because he came in here looking for trouble."

The answer did not really satisfy either of them, so they dropped the subject. Bullet and the beautiful, strange palomino horse paced side by side so that the two riders could talk in low tones without danger of anyone overhearing.

"Buck," she said suddenly, "do you have a woman of your own some place back there in Texas? I mean a wife? Do you have children?"

"No," he said without any further explanation, but she wouldn't let it rest at that.

"I don't understand it," she said. "Among the tribes a man like you would have been married long ago. The chiefs would have wanted to give you their daughters. The girls would have made advances to you till you could not help yourself. I think that even in California they would have caught you and made you a married man. So what is the matter with the women of Texas?"

"Nothing is the matter with them," Duane said. "Besides, don't be so lofty about Texas. These mountains of yours are within the boundaries of that state. That's why I'm – ."

"That's why what?"

He had meant to say, "That's why I'm here at all," and had caught himself just in time. Now he changed it to. "That's why you mustn't say it that way. You're a Texan yourself."

"Oh, no," she said. "I'm a woman of this whole wide, beautiful free land men call the West. No one state is wide enough to bound me. I belong to them all, just as I am not bound by any one of the tribes or clans of the people here."

They rode for a while in silence, savoring the hot, spiced wind that blew over the plains. She was a woman though, and could not let the subject drop.

"You dodged my question, Buck. Have you ever loved and been loved? Be honest now."

He said only, "Yes."

"Do you still love her? I must know."

"No," he said. "There is no woman back

there to whom I am bound in any way. How could there be? I was an outlaw before my twentieth year. Every man's hand turned against me. I slept in the rocks like a coyote. I was named a killer and it was a test of men's courage to try to kill me. What woman could stand that?"

"Any woman who loved you," she said simply.

They looked at each other as they rode, and there were many things unspoken except in their eyes. When they talked again it was of matters connected with the drive.

The cattle entered the foothills, moving due west. Before them towered the great bulk of the central Chisos, black and purple and overwhelming – looking ready to let slip a landslide or tumble a single peak to swallow men and beasts in one vast gulp.

Juana led them through valleys and draws and along the suddenly easy slopes of mountains. At least once each day there was water for man or beast.

"Why through here?" Duane asked her one day. "If we're heading west, isn't there a trail from the north down that side of these peaks? Why go through? Or couldn't we have just gone on south to the Rio Grande by the road we were on?"

"If there is a trail to the west," she answered, "and I'm not saying there is or isn't, the Indians close it. No herd is allowed to go that way. As far as the Rio Grande is concerned, it runs through a gorge where you would want to cross. Both banks are hundreds of feet high, and no cattle ford anywhere. Besides that part of Mexico isn't where the Old Man is going."

It was the nearest anyone had come to telling him the things Captain MacNelly and the Rangers had to know.

One crisp mountain dawn a band of Indians appeared directly ahead on the trail. By their size and the size of their horses and the way they wore feathers and paint Duane recognized them as Comanches. These firecest riders of the plains sat their horses as if man and beat were a single entity. The horses were the magnificent result of more than a century of raising and breeding.

By contrast the Apaches used scrub ponies – rode them to death and then ate them.

Juana insisted on going alone to parley with this band. From her manner Duane reckoned she had not expected the visit. The Chief came up to wait with him at the point, and he too seemed anxious and disturbed.

Behind them the restless herds milled and gave tongue to their impatience to get on with it. The rustlers herding the beasts were hard put to it to keep them under control.

The girl was gone for almost two hours – and when she returned her face and eyes were both grave. After her fashion, she got right to the point with the Old Man.

"There will be a delay," she said. "I hadn't expected it this trip, but it can't be helped. There's plenty of grass and water in the valley where we camped last night. You'll have to hold the herds there for a few days.

"And why do I have to do any such thing?"

"Because the Comanches won't let you move out," she said flatly. "There's enough of them around you here on the high ground to wipe you out and your men any time they feel like it. And believe me, they feel like it. Only a promise to me keeps the hair on your heads right this minute. As long as you stay in that valley, nothing will happen – but you'd better believe what I say and stay where I tell you."

"I've a right to know what this is all about." For the first time Duane could remember, the Old Man had lost his air of easy command. His old cheeks were flushed with concealed anger and impatience.

"In these hills," Juana said, "only those who live here have any rights at all. You don't live here. I'll tell you only this. I have to go into the mountains to see someone. It's a matter of much great importance than you and your herds. I'll be gone only a few days, but in the meantime you have to wait here for me. Either that or be eaten by the tribes. You've no other choice at all."

The outlaw fought hard for self-control. "Well, if it's only a few days."

"Better that than forever," Juana assured him. "One more thing. I'm taking Poco with me. Also I want Buck Duane and the Jackrabbit Kid. You go get him, Buck – and both of you bring your bedrolls and grub for a couple of days. Take an extra sack of white flour and coffee and sugar. Get on with it, now."

"Look here!" the Chief protested. "I don't want my men going off into those hills, with or without you. If anybody goes, it will be me."

"It will be who I say it is." For the first time there was anger in her voice. "You aren't wanted where I'm going. Go ahead, Buck. Don't waste any more time."

As Duane rode off he heard the Chief talking heatedly. The Old Man was angry. Duane would learn more of the secrets of the mountains than the Old Man wanted him to know. Juana was firm, however. When Duane and the Kid rode back, she was still refusing to even discuss the matter further.

When Poco brought up her personal things, the four of them rode off at once for the head of the valley and the waiting party of Comanche braves.

Chapter VIII

Somewhat to Buck Duane's surprise, the Indians left them as soon as the trail twisted into the woods out of sight of the men in the valley.

"We don't need them," Juana explained. "I know perfectly well where I'm going. The rest of you are as safe with me as if you were home in your own beds."

Duane rode side by side with Juana. The Kid and Poco had dropped a little way behind. "Can you tell me where you're going and why?" Duane asked.

"Of course," she said. Her face was still grave. "The Comanches brought me word I've been afraid of getting for a long time now. My father has been ill. Now he's dying and has sent for me. There's not much time, and I must go to him as fast as I can. The drive must wait."

"Of course you must," Duane said. "But why do you take me and the Kid along? We would have been safe enough back there —

that is, we would unless you've reason to think the Indians will attack."

"They won't attack unless the Old Man's a bigger fool than he looks. They'll take some beef and look haughty about it, but that's all. That isn't the reason I brought you, Buck. Father knew I was guiding a drive. He sent word that if there was a white man with the riders whom I could trust, I was to bring him with me. I can trust you, Buck."

"Yes," Duane said. "Thank you for the compliment. I won't abuse your faith. What about the Kid, though?"

"I know what you're trying to do for the Kid, Buck. Maybe this trip will help. I asked you to bring him on the chance that it would help."

"Which brings us around to you again," Duane said seriously. "I can't press you, but isn't it about time you told me who you are – and who this father of yours is? What you're doing up here in the first place? I know you're not a Comanche or Apache."

"Not yet," she said. "I can't tell you anything yet. Oh, please, Buck, don't make it any harder for me right now by trying to insist. It can't do any good. You'll know everything you've been wondering about before very long now. I promise you that I won't hold anything back when the time comes. Not a thing. Right now isn't the time, though. We have to press on as fast as we can, and just pray that I get home in time. There may not be very much time left, Buck. This has been a long while coming, but when a man reaches *lecho de muerte* he can't bargain or delay."

There was nothing more that Buck Duane could do or say.

The pace Juana set forced the horses to the limit of their endurance. The trail wound south and west and climbed higher and higher into the mountains. Sometimes it narrowed so that they had to dismount and lead their horses on a narrow shelf bordering ravines that fell away into dizzying gulfs below them.

There was no regularly marked trail – in fact, nothing in the way of evidence of prior travel that Duane could make out – and his eyes were trained by years of hunted, outlaw living in the past. Juana and Poco however moved as surely as if the way was paved and railed for every foot.

They made a dry camp that night with only the water from the canteens for themselves and their weary horses. After dark Poco made a tiny fire of long-dead twigs and branches deep in a cleft of the mountainside where it could not possibly be seen by anyone more than a few yards away.

Over this improbably small blaze he cooked their supper of fried meat and a sort of thick pancake cooked in a grease, and boiled a single small pot of coffee. They spread their bedrolls on a floor of solid rock, but in spite of this the men were weary enough to fall into deep and dreamless sleep.

Duane awoke once, well on into the night towards dawn. Juana was standing, wrapped in a heavy blanket, leaning against the wall of rock and gazing out into the gulf of darkness roofed by stars. He watched for some minutes but she did not move, and he soon fell asleep again. When he awoke once more the first gray of dawn was in the sky.

They were moving again before full daylight, and kept on hour after hour without any pause except to refill their canteens and drink the clean, icy water of a mountain rill. Horses and men began to show the strain but, young as she was, Juana was apparently tireless.

There was neither inclination nor breath for talk. Even the usually ebullient Jackrabbit Kid rode in silence, overawed by the situation in which he found himself.

Higher and higher they climbed on the flank of the great peak which Juana called 'el Casa Grande' – the great house. The way she said the words they might have meant 'the house of God.'

At last, in early afternoon, they rounded a jagged mass of rock and found themselves upon a broad, flat shelf from the other end of which the path at last turned down instead of continuing its awesome climb.

For the first time all day Juana reined her magnificent palomino, its mane and tail blowing in the cold mountain wind, and gave them time to rest and look out at the fantastic panorama spread out below their eyes.

As long as Buck Duane had lived and ridden through the West, he had to catch his breath at the view that spread before them. The Jackrabbit Kid forgot his role as outlaw and gunman, and openly gaped with his eyes round and wide and his jaw hanging open.

Even the usually masklike face of the Apache Poco showed traces of emotions which Duane could translate as love and pride. Only Juana looked out through tired and half-closed eyes that hid whatever things her heart might feel.

They were on the rim of a vast natural bowl, as if God himself had scooped a shovelful of the heart of the mountain to take away for his pleasure. The ground fell away before them for at least two thousand feet, and the opposite edge of the great depression was at least three miles away.

All round the rim the jagged peaks of native rock rose up like the stone fangs of an old Aztec sword edge. It was as if each pinnacle of stone tried to lift up its tooth above its fellows in an awful content of savage pride.

Below the slopes grew gentler and the mantle of green vegetation came to clothe the rock and warm the view to something a little less savage than a crater on the moon. The shadows marched indigo and purple, Prussian blue and black into the depths as the westering sun dropped down behind the peaks.

Far, far down in the heart of this great, silent pool of savage beauty there was a shine of water where a lake bottomed the otherwise unfloored gulf. Duane thought he could make out buildings on its shore and the rise of a plume of smoke that came up straight to meet the winds that blew it instantly to nothingness.

Juana moved her horse a step or two until they were side by side. Her hand touched his briefly. "There is my home," she said.

"It's beautiful," Duane said.

"More than beautiful, Buck. It's home . . . home! We must hurry now. Don't worry. The trail's all downhill now and wide and clearly marked."

She was right. From this point on there was a pleasant riding path looping down the slopes in long easy grades. In places there were signs that rock had been cut or blasted away and grades built up and filled.

"Your father made this road?" Duane asked.

"Not by himself," she said. "When he first came here he had helpers. They made the road – with him of course – and the hacienda, the buildings down by the lake. That was a long while ago, many years before I was born. They're all dead now, but after they died he taught the Indians to keep things up after a fashion."

"Indians?"

"Oh yes, there's an Apache clan living in here. Poco's own people, to be exact. That's why we don't have any sort of regular guard at the top of the trail. Not even a snake could slither over there without the Apaches knowing it. Though there's no danger of anyone coming up the mountain by accident. At least nobody has in all the years. He'd have to get by the Comanches and Apaches and then find that trail we came up today. I guess you could say that this is the safest place to live in all the West."

"Why did your father come here in the first place?"

"That's one of the things he'll tell you himself," she said. "That is, if he's still alive when we get home. I think he is. One of the Apaches would have met us at the rim to break the news if he'd died. They're very careful about such things. Careful and considerate among themselves in spite of what people think."

In another hour they were close enough to the lake for Duane to see the buildings Juana had referred to as the hacienda. There were several of them; some built of stone chinked with clay and others of the logs of the trees which grew in profusion on the inner slopes of the great natural bowl. All were surrounded by a breast-high wall of smaller stones and clay. There was a gate flanked by two tall cairns of stone.

The main building sat on a low elevation facing the lake and fronted by a broad verandah roofed by an extension of the main roof to the house. It looked as if it contained at least seven or eight fair-sized rooms. Immediately to the rear and joined by a roofed passage was a cookhouse. Smoke rose from the chimney in the quiet evening air.

"Poco's wife is getting us some dinner," Juana said.

There was a stable, and back of it a corral in which Duane could see two or three of the beautiful cream-and-gold palomino horses like the one Juana rode. There was no sign of the camp of the other Apaches she had spoken of.

When they were still half a mile from the gates Juana put her tired horse to a run and quickly vanished inside the big house. The Jackrabbit Kid would have followed at once but Duane held him back.

"Don't be pushy, Kid. She has a right to see her father without us crowding right at her heels. She'll tell us when we're wanted, you can be sure."

For the remaining distance they kept their horses at a slow walk, and indeed the weary beasts seemed glad enough to rest after their hard climb over the rough mountain trails earlier in the day.

After entering the unwatched gates they

all, including Poco, put their horses in the big corral and saw that they had feed and water. Only when that was done did the old Apache motion them to bring their bedrolls and supplies up to the big house. An equally ancient Indian woman came out of the cookhouse and took over the supplies they'd brought.

She was probably Poco's wife, but neither of them showed the least emotion of being reunited.

"She looks happier to see the sugar and coffee than her man," the Kid said in a low voice.

"They tell me lots of wives are like that," Duane answered him with a smile. "It takes all kinds to make a world."

Just at this moment Juana came out on the broad verandah, which Duane observed was floored with slabs of native stone, and motioned them on.

"Thank you for being so considerate," she said in a low, sweet tone. "He's still alive, though very weak. He wants to see you both right after you've eaten."

"If time's that short, we can wait till later to eat," Duane said to her.

"Oh no. That won't be necessary. He wants you to be comfortable before he sees you, and he's sure he'll live until early morning at least. He says a man so close to death can't help but know. Sarah has been cooking for us ever since we were first seen coming in, so everything is ready now."

They entered the house through a forty-by-twenty-foot living room furnished richly. Some of the furnishings, crude but strong and comfortable, had obviously been made right here in the valley. Other pieces, incongruously, showed the craft of the Eastern or even European cabinetmaker. The same incongruity recurred throughout the whole house. A gilded and scrolled mirror of the Spanish type hung over a chest of mountain oak. Fine French and English porcelain was used to serve the dinner.

It set Duane to wondering. No mountain recluse could have chosen and assembled these things, much less brought them in over the incredible mountain trails. There was a fortune in fine furnishings here, even to his untrained eye. Duane had never before seen – let alone priced – such furniture and works of art and yet he knew instinctively that Texas held nothing to match some of them, even in the homes of the great ranchers or the Governor's mansion in Austin.

His mind found only one answer – yet he hesitated to admit it even to himself. Time enough, he thought, after he'd met the owner of these things and heard the story told by his own lips in whatever way he wished to tell it.

The food was simple, but deliciously cooked. With it was served a bottle of mellow, golden Spanish wine. A fire was crackling on the broad hearth at their backs, and all three ate with good appetite after the journey of the day.

By the time they finished full night had come to the valley behind its mighty walls of stone. Here and there flickers of light upon the wooded slopes showed the location of Apache fires, and the stars hung like immense, radiant globes in the black velvet dome of sky.

Juana vanished down a long hallway while Duane smoked a fine, dark Havana cigar and the Jackrabbit looked as if he'd like to try one of the same but hesitated for fear of making a coughing, spluttering fool of himself.

"What is this place, Buck?" he asked. "How on earth did it ever get here in the middle of the back of beyond? Or am I just dreaming?"

"I know as little as you do," Duane said. "We'll find out soon enough, I think. Till then it's silly to go making wild guesses. I'm happy just to feel this good food putting strength back in my limbs. That's something you have to learn when you ride the outlaw trail, boy. Never rate anything higher than a good hot meal. You'll know that for yourself when you've roasted grasshoppers and snake meat without salt, or made a dinner of raw lizard because you daren't light a fire. It's not all riding with the Old Man's drives, you know."

The girl came back along the hallway and beckoned to them. "He wants to see you now."

They followed Juana to a great square room with floor of polished oak and windows draped in velvet to shut out the night. The light was from a fire flickering upon the hearth and candles burning in heavy Mexican silver candlesticks before a shrine which held a massive golden crucifix.

A very old Indian man squatted on his heels by the hearth and watched them with black eyes. By the paint smeared on face and body, the feathers in his hair and the medicine bags and rattles hung about his neck over the naked chest, Duane knew that this was the Apache medicine man.

The room was dominated by an immense four-poster bed carved from ebony and teak and shrouded by a tester of priceless purple velvet and brocade of gold and silver thread. In the dim light it was possible to see that an old man lay there, his body covered by soft-woven Navaho blankets, and his emaciated, almost skull-like face resting on piled pillows. Only the eyes, as blue and as bright as Juana's own, marked this as a man and not a mummy from a thousand-year-old grave.

There were chairs beside the bed and they all three sat down.

"You are welcome," a remarkably strong and melodious voice said in slightly accented English. "To the home of Don Francisco Jesus Alvarez y Luno O'Brien."

The voice ceased and the dying man waited until the pause stretched out and out. "You do not recognize the name," he said at last. "Perhaps that is as well. Let it die with me and be forgotten as I wish that I might be forgotten and . . ."

"No, Father. No," Juana said with deep emotion. "I will never forget you. Never."

For the first time since Duane had seen her she seemed on the brink of tears.

232

"Better you should forget," the old voice said. "After tonight you will wish to forget."

"Not I," she said. "It is time to tell you, Father. I know who you are. Did you think it could be kept from me all these years? I know all your secrets and I do not care."

"Not all," the man said firmly. "No one can know all but I. That is why you are here tonight, and why I asked that you bring with you these men. You must hear my story and so must others so that it may stand forever as warning to all who would err as I have erred, and sin as I have sinned."

He paused and his eyes looked at Duane. "I'm sure that Senor Duane at least is old enough to have heard my other name. Senor, you know of Captain Oberon? Of Captain Diablo Oberon? Aha. I see you do indeed."

Try as he might Duane had not been able to suppress a sudden start of horror and repulsion as he remembered half-understood tales of his childhood. There was not a Texan in those days who had not heard of the Captain Oberon, most merciless and deadly of all the white chiefs of the renegade Comancheros. No one, it was said, had seen his face as captive or enemy and returned to tell the tale.

This was the legendary master of evil who had become a faceless horror riding out of the Staked Plains at the head of a wild band of red and white fiends to raid and burn and kill. For year after year his name had struck terror to Mexican vaquero and Texan borderer alike. In the end he had vanished in some horrible and nameless fashion that had made men say, "His master the Devil came and took him away."

This, then, was the old man who lay so still upon the great carved bed? This was Juana's beloved father? Buck Duane did not know what to do or say.

"You will listen, then, Senores," the dying man said. "There is no padre here to shrive my soul, but I must speak it out at last. You will listen – and if you cannot understand or pardon, I will not blame you."

THE COMANCHERO'S STORY

I was born, Senores, a grandee of Spain and Mexico. There is no better nor more noble blood than flows in my dear daughter's veins. How then do I come here?

I was born also with a taint of pride and cruelty that came to dominate the rest of me to such an extent that all the decent and human impulses were shut out. At an early age my sins had become so well known in Spain that the King banished me to our family estates in Mexico for life. My father wept to see me go, but spoke no word to protest a sentence which he well knew to be just.

It was not long before even the frontier republic of Mexico became too hot to hold me. Our family holdings there were extensive, but not rich. There had been a silver mine, long since worked out. The life of a ranchero was too tame for me. I gambled, blustered and dueled until my enemies were too many and too powerful for me to show my face in the Valley of Mexico.

Greed and arrogance drove me to the frontier and to the wild, mad lands beyond. I was taken and tortured by Comanches. I laughed in their faces, challenged their chief to combat and slew him with my naked hands.

The bloody warriors admired such exploits and recognized me as one of their own in spirit if not in the flesh. I was adopted into the tribe and soon gained the fame and status of a war band chief. Wild spirits – Indian, Mexican, and a few American –

flocked to my command, drawn by the greed of gold and the legend of my invincibility.

In the war of Texan Independence I was Santa Anna's ally. When the Americans fought Mexico, I raided both armies alike. Neither Texan ranch and homestead nor Mexican ranchero, mine and village were safe from my raids after that. I sold captives into slavery, burned and slew. There was no crime or sin I scorned.

I used the paths through these mountains to raid and to bring home my loot. The torture fires of my braves burned where this house now stands. In my arrogance and sinful pride I cursed the name of God. Because of my education and knowledge of the outside world I became business agent for the Comancheros of other bands. I had allies among the merchants of Mexico and of Peru and England and Spain. I had business associates in Havana and New Orleans, New York and Lisbon and London. I was known and feared under a dozen names in the capitals of the world.

Yet always greed and lust and the demonic cruelty within me drew me back to this wild, God-cursed frontier of savagery, rapine and death. Or perhaps it was God himself who knew that I had grown too evil for the world without.

I thought that I had grown invulnerable – but, alas, no man is that. My last and bloodiest raid was over thirty years ago.

I had struck deep into the Texas settlements, and my band was rich with slaves and cattle, fine horses, weapons and trade goods. We came south and west of this very peak and crossed into Mexico at a point close to the place where the Rio Grande plunges into its wild ravines.

It was there that disaster struck. The Mexican authorities had been alerted by a traitor in my band. Their cavalry struck us in force when half our train was still in the river ford. American cavalry working with the Mexicans came down on the rear of our column. It was not a battle but a wild and bloody rout.

Some of my warriors, a band of captives, and a herd of stolen horses alone broke free. I led them in wild flight into the high mountains of northern Mexico. At first the Federales were close on our heels and there was bloody rear-guard actions in which the last of our wagons of loot were lost.

It was then that still more terrible forces appeared to harry the remnant of our band.

The Yaqui Indians, sworn enemy to Comanche and Apache, came down upon us in force. We fought them off with heavy losses to both sides and fled ever deeper into the wild and trackless peaks. They came hot on our heels. The Mexican cavalry dared not follow where we went, but the clans of the Yaqui gathered for the kill.

Winter was on us then – and in those barren piles of naked rocks its cold and terror was magnified a hundred times.

We found a valley with water and wood. It was really just a mighty knife cut in the hills, but there was only one narrow pass to let men in and out. The Yaqui watched one end and we the other. This was journey's end.

We ate the few deer in the desolate valley – and the horses we had driven in. We ate our horses and the bark of trees.

Among the captives was a young and beautiful American girl who had been captured on her way to marry a frontier preacher in Texas. She nursed us like a saint and cared for us. She was alive only because I had saved her for my own vile purposes.

In the end there was nothing more to eat – except ourselves!

Shrink back in horror if you will, young men. There is an awful time of decision in which the lust to live will overrule all things. I do not seek to excuse, only to tell what we did.

In frenzy of madness we ate first the prisoners, all except the woman captive, who was to become your mother, and then the weakest ones of our own band. I would not let them eat your mother and I was still the strongest of them all. They looked on me with superstitious fear. El Captain Diablo was devil indeed in those awful weeks.

Of us all, only your mother-to-be would not eat human flesh. She lived on mosses and small creeping things caught with incredible patience, and the boiled leather of harness and shoes. She grew thin as a skeleton, and never really recovered from those things.

At last, creeping among the rocks in search of food, she found a way to scale the canyon cliffs. Those of us who lived still – and we were few – followed that precarious way to freedom and fled north across the terrible and barren peaks. Some sickened on the way, and we left them where they fell to die. In the Spring, the Yaquis found the bodies in the canyon and decided devils must have come to carry off the rest of us. That place is still forbidden ground.

In the end a few of us won back to this place, and here you, Juana, were born. The Apaches befriended us and kept our secret well. I sent you out to be educated and brought you here at other times. You know the rest and can tell the Senores at leisure.

The old man's face was livid. His breath came in gasps, and he seemed on the point of death. One claw-like hand reached forth.

"You must forgive me, my child, so that I may die. Forgiveness of man I cannot expect. That of God I dare not even ask, but yours I must have."

"You had it long ago, my father," she said in heartfelt tones.

"No, no. You could not forgive what you did not yet know. My child, you are not the child of love. Your mother could not love me though I sought to win her. At last I took her for my own by force, and from that hellish union you became the fruit. It was at your birth she died."

"I forgive you, Father," the girl said.

"Observe, Senores," The old man went on, "the end of pride and arrogance and lust and greed. Observe strength drained and skill made useless and all violence brought down to nothing on this bed.

"For year upon year I lived on here while all my comrades died before my eyes. In all those years I longed above anything else to return to the world I had so carelessly cast aside in the days of my youth. I could not even hope to go weep upon my blessed mother's grave. I could seek no help from priest or church. I was forever outlawed and forever damned and this valley only a special hell that God had made to hold me. There is treasure here to rouse the envy of a king, and at any moment I would have given it all – to the last scudo – for a chance to walk a city's streets again as a man among men. But I could never go forth. This valley was my tomb. I was forever and ever cut off from all humanity.

"Go now, when I have died, and let my story be told. Take my dear Juana with you if she wishes to go. This house and this retreat and all that I have gathered here is hers. Do not seek to take anything hence for yourselves. The Apaches will stop you.

"One last thing, Senores. If ever it is in your hearts, speak to a priest for me and say I beg his prayers. Say that I seek only a prayer for a soul that is forever damned."

It was all that he could say. The skull-like head fell back upon the pillow, and, though life remained, its light now flickered only dimly in his breast.

The Indian shaman pressed a cup of some dark and stinking liquid to the thin lips and the old man swallowed a few drops. Juana was weeping and her body shook with uncontrollable sobs.

Chapter IX

The Jackrabbit Kid sat as if paralyzed by what he had heard. Duane got to his feet and shook the Kid's shoulders until he had attracted his attention. They went out together and closed the door softly on that room of horror and of sadness.

Back in the big living room the fire had been built up to last the night. There were comfortable chairs and bottles of whiskey, brandy and wine set out, and a silver box of the good Havana cigars. The old Comanchero had lacked for no luxury in all his years of exile. The things that he needed had been bought abroad by agents of Juana and passed from hand to hand, from Mexican to Indian and at last to this hidden place.

Buck Duane would have preferred to be alone with his thoughts, but the Jackrabbit Kid wouldn't have it that way.

"Lord, Buck," he said, "do you think that old man really did all the things he said?"

"He said so, boy. Why else do you suppose he did that unless they're true? Dying men don't play games."

"If he did, I'm not sorry for him. All that killing and evil and eating his own men. I don't understand how a human being could . . ." The boy's voice trailed off in sheer horror.

"You better understand," Duane said suddenly and with an intensity that brought the boy up in his chair. "Don't you get it, Kid? Don't you see? You wear that gun and you ride big with rustlers and killers. You say you're an outlaw, and you want to stay an outlaw? Don't you?"

"I've got to, Buck. I killed a man."

"Got to, nothing. You killed a man nobody heard of in a town ain't even on the map. In self-defense too. What does that do – make you Jesse James? Not unless you want it to, it doesn't. You got your eyes full of stars and your head full of adventure. That's what you've got, isn't it?"

"But, Buck . . . you . . . I mean . . . Here I am and . . ."

"And a fine fool you're making of yourself, Kid, sitting here acting shocked by what that man says. Don't you know who he is? He's yourself, Kid, in another sixty years

244

if you get to the top of the road you've picked for yourself. That's no two-bit rustler like Jerry Link, nor no business operator like the Old Man. In there on that bed lies the king of them all. That's el Captain Diablo, the devil's brother-in-law, the man whose name the murdering hill 'Paches use to scare their kids with. He's got treasure to buy St. Louis if he wants it. No man dared go against him when he rode, and now he's lying in his bed."

"But, Buck – eating his own men!"

"You want to be a real outlaw, Kid? Then you better be ready to eat your own mother if need be. You better be ready to anything that a man did and more – not for treasure and a castle like this, but just to stay alive. Just to hide in the rocks like a snake, boy, and freeze in the winter like a sore-legged mangy coyote. Just to know that no man on earth will hesitate to kill you if he can. You think about all that, Kid, before and go condemning an old man lying in there waiting for Satan to come pluck him off his deathbed. You hear me, now."

After a long pause. "You sound like you liked him, Buck."

"No, Kid," Duane said. "I don't like him. I hate his guts. His and Bill Bonney's, and

Jeff Harper's, and Jesse James' and the rest. I hate them because they put glamour on the gun and a youngster like you don't see it till too late. I hate them for that, but as to that old man, I do something else . I understand him.."

One of the big logs on the fire cracked like a gunshot and sent a golden shower of sparks dancing up the flue.

"I understand him, Kid. You think about that. It could be me on that bed in there. It could be you, less'n we both die in the rocks. You think it out."

They both sat for a long while watching the fire burn low and busy with their own thoughts. Sometimes Duane dozed, but he knew that the alertness cultivated through long years of living as a hunted man would rouse him at the slightest unusual sound.

So it was. In the time of deepest sleep, just before the flash of dawn ran over the rim of this hidden valley, he heard the girl's light step at the far end of the passage and came full awake.

She paused in the doorway and looked at them. She had been weeping, but now her eyes were dry. She held her head up with a curious mixture of mature pride and childish defiance.

Duane came to his feet. Behind him the Kid slept on with his head on the back of the chair and his mouth open.

Juana put out her hand and then let it drop at her side. "It's over," she said. "A few minutes ago. He struggled terribly for life at the end, but he did not cry out."

She paused and looked at the Ranger with a mixture of doubt, perplexity and fear in her beautiful eyes. "I suppose," she said. "I mean, now, after what you heard, you'll think . . ."

"You mean," Duane said, "that maybe I'll condemn him and shrink away from his daughter. That was his life, Juana. You and I mightn't want to copy him, but I can understand it. It has nothing to do with you."

He took her in his arms and kissed her very gently on the forehead. It was all the moment allowed, and it was enough. She clung to his tall figure and wept against his shoulder.

Behind them the Kid slept on.

Late in the morning all three ate a breakfast of steaks, eggs and corn cakes washed down with coffee strong enough to stand a spoon in.

The old Comanchero's body had been

taken up into the hills by the Apaches to be buried in a secret place.

"It was his wish," Juana explained. "Even I am not to know exactly where he is. For years he's been afraid that the descendants of the people he wronged long ago would find his body and desecrate the grave. To me this whole valley will always be his home – living or dead."

A transformed Poco in ceremonial paint and a white buckskin jacket beaded with sacred symbols had led the warriors who took the corpse away. At first the men had hardly recognized him when he passed.

"Who is Poco?" the Kid asked.

"That's only the name we use for him when we got out of the mountains," Juana said. "His real name is Vibora and he was the first of father's war chiefs."

Duane knew the name as that of the boldest, cruelest and most famous of the old-time terrors of the frontier. "I called him a one-man army once," he said. "I guess I was right, for sure."

"Have you always lived here?" Duane said after the Kid had gone out to the corral to look at the palominos. "I mean, what are your plans now? How will you manage?"

"That will be easy enough," she

answered. "Father never wanted me to grow up as an Indian. You know I was educated in California. Besides that I've gone in and out of here for years. Years ago Father established bank accounts and business agents in Europe and New York and New Orleans. He has treasure here, buried somewhere.

"I suppose Poco will show me later on. It was only the least of his fortune. He established me as his heir and business representative some while ago. The truth is, Buck, I can live anywhere in the world I really want to."

"Then why? I don't mean why come back here, but why act as guide for a rustler band?"

"It was Father's idea. The years had changed him, but he was still a bandit and a greedy one at heart. When the Old Man first got the idea of running his herds this way, the Comanches brought us the news. They wanted to wipe him out, but Father said no. He sent me with the war chief to make a bargain. We'd give him safe passage and guard him and guide him out again. In return he gave beef and guns to the Indians and brought in supplies to us.

"It appealed both to Father's greed and

his sense of humor. Besides it supplied the Indians with things they wanted and helped keep them from raiding and drawing attention to this place. If we'd kept the Old Man out completely, others might have come after him and found out the secret of the Chisos."

"Where does he take the beef?"

This was the question that had led Captain MacNelly to send Buck Duane into the badlands in the first place. He held his breath waiting for the answer. When it came his heart sank again, for it took him not one step further.

"I honestly don't know, Buck. Oh, I take him out to the west over the old Comanchero trails. I know them all, and I try to double him around and confuse him as much as I can every trip. In the end I take him out of the badlands onto fairly open ground somewhere between the Pecos and the Rio Grande. I know he has buyers who meet him there after I leave, but whether they're Mexican or American and where they take the stock I don't know. There must be a changing of brands, but after that the beef could go north, west or south. It's never been any of my affair, so I haven't troubled to find out."

"What are you going to do now?" Duane asked to hide his disappointment.

"Go on back and take him through, I guess," she answered. "I don't really want to, of course, but I can't see anyway out. I don't even dare leave the drive where it is more than another day or so. They'd be sure to pick a quarrel with the Comanches, and if they did, not a man of them would ever get out of the trap they're in. No – I'll see them through this time, but not again."

"Won't the Comanches be upset at losing their beef and the rest of the toll the rustlers pay?"

"If they are, they can guide him through themselves. Anyway that's what I'll tell the Old Man."

"He won't be happy about it," Duane said. "By the way, who is he, really?"

"I know that," she said. "I found out from some of my outside business connections soon after this whole thing started. His name, though he's used a lot of them in his time, is really Virgil Dawson. He was a cotton broker in New Orleans before the War, a blockade runner and then crooked contractor and scalawag under the Reconstruction government. When his deals began to smell too high for the city, he came west. No matter what he touches, he gets rich. Buck, I'm going to have to ask you and the Kid not to tell him anything of what you've seen and heard of this trip."

"I'll answer for both of us," Duane said.

"Thanks. I hope it won't make trouble for you."

"No more than I have anyway," Duane said. "I'm sure a mind like Dawson's will suspect you and me of all sorts of double dealing on this trip. I'll try to convince him it was just a sort of honeymoon, if you'll forgive me."

"That's what I wish it had been," she said forthrightly, "and well you know it. But all that can wait. My father isn't buried yet."

He took her hand and held it and a current of life and desire ran hot between them.

Chapter X

The following morning Poco came back out of the hills in his usual ragged garb, and the four of them left the hidden valley of the Chisos range. The ride was all downhill this time, and much easier on the horses. They could have made Dawson's camp by late evening, but preferred to camp on the trail so as to come in after daylight.

It was that night that Juana and Buck Duane opened their hearts to each other under blazing Western stars.

Toward morning he told her his story – his whole story including the outlaw years and his present status as a member of Captain MacNelly's company of Texas Rangers. He assured her that it was only the Old Man and his buyers to the west who would be turned in to the law.

"Once he's taken and the rustling broken up," Duane said, "there'll be no reason to interfere with the Indian's life in this secluded valley."

When she understood, Juana was frankly delighted. "Oh Buck," she said. "Somehow I knew you were too fine a man – too strong and decent – to be an outlaw and a hunted man. Now I can truly love you."

When they rode out of the cover of the trees in the morning and saw the trail camp with breakfast fires smoking and the herds grazing in the valley, Buck Duane was ready for whatever might come. He knew that the Chief would never believe that he and Juana had not been plotting to take the secret route away from him. His mind simply would not credit that they had not.

Duane's death – 'execution' the Chief would probably call it – must have been already decided upon. The only question in Duane's mind was when and how the attempt would be made. That it would be was as certain as that night follows day.

The way Duane saw it, the Old Man wouldn't try anything right away. He would figure Duane and Juana were in cahoots. If he killed one – unless, of course, he could make it look like an accident – he would have to kill the other, too. That would leave him without a guide.

Of course, he might figure he could find his way out without the girl. It was possible he could – except for the Comanches and Apaches. If their friend were killed, the tribes would come down on the herd like wolves.

For all these reasons Duane felt he would be reasonably safe until the herds were in open country and close to Dawson's rendezvous with his buyers. That is, except for the possibility of an 'accident' or an uncontrollable rage on Dawson's part.

He had told a little of this to Juana when they were alone the night before – not that he was certain the attack would be made, but only enough to alert her. He didn't want her bringing down the Indians before he'd managed to get the facts the Rangers needed.

As soon as they were sighted a rider broke away from the herds and came up at a gallop. It proved to be Bart.

"Am I glad to see you, Boss," he said as soon as Duane reined up. "Old fancy pants has been like to blow his cork for two days watching for you. The whole camp's wondering what he's so hot about. That is all but a half dozen of his personal gunslingers that he's been talking to private-like."

"It's the kind of ranny he is," Duane said. "Always jealous of the other fellow."

"You can't blame him," Bart said, looking over at Juana. "Anyway, Boss, it looks like trouble. What I want you to know is, if it comes to a showdown I'm with you. We won't be alone either by the looks of things. His high-and-mighty lordship ain't too popular with the boys. Him an' his bodyguards an' special grub an' whiskey an' all. Even that fancy half-Mex of la Jim Dancer come to me quiet-like the other day. Tell you to watch the wind close, he says."

"Thanks, Bart," Duane said with real sincerity. "Believe me, I appreciate the way you feel and you won't suffer for it. Not while Buck Duane can still pull trigger, you won't, and that'll be for years to come. I don't think there'll be any blowoff today. Keep your eyes and ears open and pass the word along I'll stand by any man who stands by me. Let the boys know, too, that we can bring the Indians in on our side. That should make them think."

"I get you," Bart said. "You can count on me."

"Fine. Get me a tally, if you can, of the men who ride with us."

The Old Man and several of his bodyguard of gunmen had started to walk out from the camp towards the little group of riders. Buck Duane and Juana spurred their horses and the girl waved a greeting. The rustlers stopped and waited for them.

A short way from the group, Buck dismounted and tossed his reins to Poco. If there was to be a showdown he wanted solid ground under his feet and both hands free. A couple of the herders saw what was up and started to ride over. This was the outlaw's chance to gun down Duane and seize the girl for a hostage, if he was desperate enough to try it.

Juana must have had the same idea. She sprang down from the palomino and ran out between the two groups calling out, "Hold on. Let's talk this over."

The big rattler came up out of the grass ahead of her, its wicked triangular head waving to and from on a thick neck and the rattles whirring menace. She tried to stop, but it was too late. The hideous mouth opened to show wicked fangs as the big snake struck.

Duane's hand blurred into motion so swift that no eye could follow. The Colt .45 seemed to leap into his hand of its own violition and the hammer fell even as the muzzle swung level. With the crash of the shot the headless body of the snake fell back to lash convulsively at the girl's very feet.

She turned white and would have fallen except for Duane's strong arm about her waist.

The oncoming riders, the gunmen, and the people around Duane all stared with unbelieving eyes.

"My God," said one of the gunslingers. "It ain't true. It can't be true even if I saw it. No man living can out-draw a striking snake. It just can't be."

"He did it," the Jackrabbit Kid yelled to the riders and the world in general. "He let the snake strike and drew and killed it before the fangs hit! No gun ever equalled that before."

Buck Duane put his gun back in the holster. It wouldn't be needed now, and everyone there knew it. The men behind Dawson were tough professional killers, but not one of them would face that fabulous draw.

"We'll go in and talk," Dawson said. "It's time this herd moved out of here."

All round the rim of the valley little knots of Comanche riders had come out of the woods. Watching the camp, they'd seen that shot. When Buck Duane stepped forward they raised their rifles and lances in salute and wild whoops sounded in applause.

Chapter XI

In four more days the riders drove their stolen stock down the last foothills of the Chisos range and out on the the comparatively open plains. It was here they saw the last of the Comanches who had watched their flanks every step of the way. Half-naked, painted and whooping young braves brought their ponies into camp at a dead run to collect the beeves, horses, guns and boxes of ammunition and supplies promised them for a safe passage.

They departed presently, yelling their contempt of the white men who paid rather than fought them.

With them went Juana and Poco.

She had protested bitterly to Duane. "Can't leave you alone, and I won't. That wicked old man is full of hatred for you. He won't rest till he kills you. I know it, and I could not bear that."

Duane had laughed and tried to seem perfectly unconcerned. "The rattler robbed him of his chance to kill me," he said. "There's not a gunman on his payroll that would face me in a fight after that. Besides half the men – maybe more – would take my part in a fight anyhow."

"Then why stay with that stupid drive, Buck? Come back to the valley with me, dear. There is safety and peace for a time. If we want to leave later on, there is money enough to go anywhere in the world that we please. There. A woman can't speak plainer than that."

She kissed him passionately, and he returned her kiss.

"I can't," he said flatly. "God knows I want to, Juana. I must finish this drive, and you know why. I made that promise to captain MacNelly before I ever knew that you were alive, let alone that we loved each other."

"You can trust me, Buck."

"I know – and this time you must trust me. Go back to the valley and wait for me. When what I have to do is finished, I will come and tell you about it. I promise you that."

She could not shake him and she was too proud to plead, so she rode out of camp with the Comanches. Just before she left, she had

261

a talk with Dawson and he made her promise to wait word from him and guide future herds through as in the past. Neither of them believed what they said, but this was a matter of form. As long as they had the talk there was no open break, and they were free to deal with the future as might seem best to each of them.

For Duane's part, he felt that his job was almost done. He was sincere when he told Juana he didn't think the Chief would dare make an open attempt to have him killed. The odds were too evenly balanced if fighting broke out in the band. Besides, no matter who won such a fight, it would ruin the Old Man's whole carefully worked out setup.

It was more likely Dawson would wait to see if his suspicions were correct. If he could not get through the Chisos route another time, then he might hire men to seek out and kill Duane.

Duane planned to finish the drive. Once he knew who the buyers were, he'd head back for the valley. Juana said the Indians would let him through. Then they'd go back to Texas together and he could give Captain MacNelly all the facts he needed to keep Dawson or any other rustler from using that route again. The mountain Indians needn't be bothered as long as they refrained from raiding down into Texas or otherwise provoking official reprisals.

His plan was to leave the drive as soon as he had definite proof of the identity of the buyers and the market where they in turn took the herds.

He hadn't long to wait. Dawson put the herds into a sheltered valley close to where Juana had left them and sent off one of his bodyguards on a fast horse to go ahead. All the other men were told to stay in camp. Men were coming to take over the herd, and they'd be paid off at that time.

Buck Duane knew that they were somewhere south of a line from the tiny settlement of Marathon to Fort Davis. A short drive would put the stolen animals on well-traveled trails going west or north. A hard turn to the south would put them over the Rio Grande into Texas. From the direction in which the rider had gone, he figured the new buyers would come from Fort Davis. Meanwhile there was nothing to do but wait.

He kept the Jackrabbit Kid close to him at all times on the pretext that "I need somebody I can trust to watch my back,

Kid. A man hasn't eyes in the back of his skull."

Mostly he wanted to be sure Dawson didn't grab the Kid and try to make him tell what had happened in the mountains. The Kid would be loyal, and get himself tortured as a result. Duane was worried anyway. Now the Kid followed him out of a boy's hero worship. What would his reaction be when he found out Duane was a Texas Ranger? That's when the youngster would really be put to the test. A boy is unpredictable as wind – Duane knew it and it worried him.

About noon of the third day in camp Dawson's bodyguard brought the buyers in. There were two of them, hard-bitten characters in long black frock-coats and Stetson hats. Each man also had a bodyguard sporting two guns and carrying Winchester rifles across their saddles. The men led a pack horse which quite evidently carried the coin and banknotes to pay off for the herds. They rode straight for Dawson's tent.

The Old Man's crew gathered around the tent in a big circle as close as they dared come. They knew the payoff was imminent and the money drew them like a magnet.

Jim Dancer came out and talked to them. The buyer's drovers would be along later in the day to relieve them. Any who wanted could sign on with the new leaders for the rest of the drive, as they were short of hands. The buyers were called Miller and Dongan.

They were taking the herd all the way to California, dropping off small bunches as they could be sold along the way at Army posts and towns and to ranchers needing stock. A couple of days drive would get them out of Texas to safety.

The rest would go north with the Old Man to intersect the Goodnight-Loving trail. They'd be paid off in Colorado.

Duane knew what that meant. Dawson was afraid to pay off his men till he got them out of Texas. They'd head straight for the saloons and fancy houses and some might talk.

The men didn't like the idea of a delayed payoff. There was a howl of protest. "We want our money. We earned it and we want it now. Give us our money."

Dancer tried to argue with the men, but they wouldn't listen to him. Guns were waved in the air. Finally Dancer went back into the tent for a conference.

Dawson's personal following of gunmen

drew into a circle around the tent. There were eight of them besides the two guards who had come with Dongan and Miller. Outside their ring almost forty men yelled for their money. Only a few of them were real gunslingers, but all were armed and looking for trouble.

Loud voices came from the tent. Apparently the buyers were telling Dawson to pay off and stop the uproar. They'd come to buy cattle, not to fight for their lives.

Dawson came out by himself.

"All right," he yelled. "Let's talk it over before somebody gets hurt. Back off a ways and my boys will too."

The men backed off about fifty yards. The gunmen, except for Dawson's bodyguards and the two strange bodyguards went the same distance in the other direction. They stood facing each other and trying to decide what to do next.

"Send Buck Duane in," one of the men suggested. "He cant talk for us – him and that snake-killing gun!"

The last thing Duane wanted was to become totally involved at this point. He had what he'd come for and wanted to get clear with the information. But the men demanded it and there was nothing he could

266

do. The Kid insisted on going with him.

"Remember your back, Buck," he said.

As Duane walked forward he saw that the men waiting for him had split into two groups. On his left, and a little in advance of the others stood the Old Man and one of his body servants. The black had a shotgun tucked loosely under his arm. The Chief showed no guns, but Duane figured him for at least a couple of hidden derringers, probably one in a forearm clip under his shirt.

About thirty feet to the right and a little behind these two Dongan and Miller and their two hired guns stood in a loose grouping. They were actually out of the conference and only there as observers.

Duane walked easily, letting his hands swing at the end of his arms, but never letting them get far from his gun butts. Walking into such a setup was always a little like smoking over an open keg of gunpowder. He didn't really expect trouble, but long years on the outlaw trail had taught the Ranger that the price of life was all too often eternal vigilance.

As he came forward he heard one of the buyers' gunslingers say to his boss, "Mr.

Miller, I've seen that man some place before."

Every nerve in Duane's body tightended to the killing pitch. The icy knot that came before crucial and sudden action was in his stomache. Adrenalin poured into the blood.

"You might have, Tom," Miller was saying. "They say he's fast. He's the one they said shot the snake, I think."

Duane's hands poised almost on the butts of his two guns. He sensed what was coming next. Because of that, he'd have the edge he needed. The trouble was there were two groups. He couldn't watch and fire at both at once. No man living could.

The man Tom watched him intently. "I know I've seen him," he said. "I've seen him kill a man." Suddenly he started. "My God, Boss, that's the Ranger killed Tulsa Harrow. I saw him."

For a second everybody froze. Then the Old Man yelled, "Ranger! Kill him, boys! Cut him down!"

Duane made his life-and-death decision in a split second. The Old Man and his personal bodyguards weren't professional guns. The two men with the buyers were. He'd have to take them first, trust that the buyers were slow and try to get Dawson and the shotgunner next. It was an impossible gamble, but not to try was certain death.

He walked on in and the guns bloomed flowers of flame in his hands. The man Tom was fast but he never reached his gun. Duane's first shot cut him down.

His sidekick was a shade slower to react, and that meant he never had a chance. The second and third slugs from Duane's right-hand gun sounded almost as one report. The slugs punched out his right lung and heart.

The two buyers were businessmen, not killers. They bought their corpses instead of making them. They started to put their hands in the air.

Duane saw movement flicker out of the corner of his eye where one of Dawson's bodyguards brought the shotgun around. He tried desperately to turn head and arm for a left-hand shot. The buckshot would cut him in two at that range. Every muscle pulled with tigerish strength to pull him round even as he knew the best he could do was a dead heat.

Behind him a .45 thundered once and again. The big bodyguard came straight erect with the impact of the first slug. The second slammed him over on his back. Both barrels of the slug gun fired uselessly into the sky.

Dawson was trying for his derringer, but it was snagged on his linen cuff. When he saw Buck Duane's guns come round to him, he opened his hands and squealed for help like a goat caught under a fence. Then he put his hands up as the buyers already had.

Both the Chief's gunmen and the rustlers behind Duane had been too far away to hear the accusing cry of "Ranger!" All they knew was that killing had started. The two groups milled and yelled.

Buck Duane turned to his three prisoners. "If one of you opens his mouth, he's dead," he said. "Watch them, Kid."

Then he turned to wave to both gunmen and rustlers. He raised his voice to a shout they could hear. "It's all over, boys. The money's in the tent there. Go get it."

Both groups understood the logic of that. They ran for the tent. Under the rush it went down. Men trapped inside fought blindly to reach the money bags, while those outside tried to get the canvas off. Hostility between the groups were forgotten. Even the herders in the valley came galloping up, leaving the stolen stock to mill aimlessly about.

Duane and the Kid herded their disarmed

prisoners over to the remuda where saddled horses were picketed. Bullet came to Duane's whistle. The others took what horses they could.

"Ride for the hills," Buck Duane ordered. "We're taking you back the way you came."

They hadn't far to go. At the very crest of the valley they were met by a wave of whooping Comanche braves whom Juana had been holding to watch the camp – "In case any harm came to Buck."

Juana joined them with a picked guard of Indians. The rest took the unguarded cattle and horses out of the valley with a single screeching rush while the rustlers were still fighting each other for the cash in the tent.

"We'll take these fellows back to face Texas law," Buck Duane told Juana. "Captain MacNelly will arrange that this is the last of the 'invisible' drives. Nobody will repeat what the Chief started ever."

"What about me?" the Jackrabbit Kid said. "I killed a man."

"I think you wiped the score clean this time," Duane said. "Captain MacNelly will think the same. He's that kind of man, and the Rangers have friends in this end of Texas. We'll get you a verdict of self-defense, and you can ride like a man again."

The Kid grinned from ear to ear. "I'll go for that," he said. Then his face changed. "Why didn't you tell me before you could do that?"

"I wanted to see if you were a man," Duane said. "A man makes his own decisions for himself. Just like you did when you saved a Ranger's life."

He rode ahead with Juana, Bullet matching the palomino stride for stride in a magnificent and joyous burst of speed.

Zane Grey Westerns
In Large Print

CODE OF THE WEST

THE FUGITIVE TRAIL

THE HERITAGE OF THE DESERT

ROBBERS' ROOST

STRANGER FROM THE TONTO

THE TRAIL DRIVER

TO THE LAST MAN

WEST OF THE PECOS

Frank Roderus Westerns
in Large Print

COWBOY

JOURNEY TO UTAH

OLD KYLE'S BOY